"I wrote my first short story when I was seventeen and wrote dozens more before any of them were accepted for publication. Luckily most of these stories have been lost. I switched to plays and they were worse. Finally, after World War II, at the age of twenty-eight, I started my first novel. I knew immediately that this was what I wanted to do for the rest of my life."

—MARIO PUZO

First published under a pseudonym in 1967, *Six Graves to Munich* was Mario Puzo's literary predecessor to his legendary novel, *The Godfather*. In this unsung classic, Puzo's trademark unflinchingly stark writing style, vivid descriptive skill, and relentless pace are exemplified in the genre of the spy novel. In his hands, the classic tale of revenge becomes a haunting study of humanity at its most visceral, offering a glimpse into a damaged soul whose only remaining purpose for living is to kill.

SIX GRAVES TO MUNICH

MARIO PUZO

WRITING AS

Mario Cleri

NAL NEW AMERICAN LIBRARY

NEW AMERICAN LIBRARY
Published by New American Library,
a division of Penguin Group (USA) Inc.,
375 Hudson Street, New York, New York 10014, USA
Penguin Group (Canada), 90 Eglinton Avenue East, Suite 700, Toronto,
Ontario M4P 2Y3, Canada (a division of Pearson Penguin Canada Inc.)
Penguin Books Ltd., 80 Strand, London WC2R 0RL, England
Penguin Ireland, 25 St. Stephen's Green, Dublin 2,
Ireland (a division of Penguin Books Ltd.)
Penguin Group (Australia), 250 Camberwell Road, Camberwell,
Victoria 3124, Australia (a division of Pearson Australia Group Pty. Ltd.)
Penguin Books India Pvt. Ltd., 11 Community Centre,
Panchsheel Park, New Delhi - 110 017, India
Penguin Group (NZ), 67 Apollo Drive, Rosedale, North Shore 0632,
New Zealand (a division of Pearson New Zealand Ltd.)
Penguin Books (South Africa) (Pty.) Ltd., 24 Sturdee Avenue,
Rosebank, Johannesburg 2196, South Africa

Penguin Books Ltd., Registered Offices:
80 Strand, London WC2R 0RL, England

Published by New American Library, a division of Penguin Group (USA) Inc.
Published by arrangement with the Estate of Mario Puzo.

First New American Library Printing, May 2010
1   3   5   7   9   10   8   6   4   2

Copyright © Mario Puzo, 1967
All rights reserved

 REGISTERED TRADEMARK—MARCA REGISTRADA

Set in Palatino
Designed by Elke Sigal

Printed in the United States of America

PUBLISHER'S NOTE
This is a work of fiction. Names, characters, places, and incidents either are the product of the author's imagination or are used fictitiously, and any resemblance to actual persons, living or dead, business establishments, events, or locales is entirely coincidental.

The publisher does not have any control over and does not assume any responsibility for author or third-party Web sites or their content.

SIX GRAVES TO MUNICH

CHAPTER 1

M ichael Rogan checked the lurid sign outside Hamburg's hottest nightclub. *Sinnlich! Schamlos! Sündig!* Sensual! Shameless! Sinful! The Roter Peter made no bones about what it was selling. Rogan took a small photograph out of his pocket and studied it by the red light of the swine-shaped door lamp. He had studied the photograph a hundred times, but he was nervous about recognizing the man he was looking for. People changed a great deal in ten years, Rogan knew. He himself had changed.

He went past the obsequiously bowing doorman into the club. Inside it was dark except for the "blue" movie flickering on a small rectangular screen. Rogan threaded his way through the crowded tables, the noisy, alcohol-stinking crowd. Suddenly the house lights came on and framed him against the stage, with naked blond girls dancing above his head. Rogan's eyes searched the faces of those seated at ringside tables. A waitress touched his arm. She said coquettishly in German, "Is the Herr Amerikaner looking for something special?"

Rogan brushed past her, annoyed at being so easily spotted as an American. He could feel the blood pounding against the silver plate that held his skull together—a danger signal. He would have to do this job quickly and get back to his hotel. He moved on through the club, checking the dark corners, where patrons drank beer from huge steins and impersonally grabbed at the nearest waitress. He glanced into the curtained booths, where men sprawled on leather sofas and studied the girls on stage before picking up the phone to summon their favorite to join them.

Rogan was becoming impatient now. He didn't have much more time. He turned and faced the stage. Behind the nude dancing girls there was a transparent panel in the curtain. Through the panel the patrons could see the next line of girls getting ready to go on stage, and they applauded every time one of the girls took off a bra or a stocking. A voice called out drunkenly, "You darlings, ah, you darlings—I can love you all."

Rogan turned toward the voice and smiled in the darkness. He remembered that voice. Ten years had not changed it. It was a fatty, choking Bavarian voice, thick with false friendliness. Rogan moved swiftly toward it. He opened his jacket and slipped off a leather button that gripped the Walther pistol securely in its shoulder holster. With his other hand he took the silencer out of his jacket pocket and held it as if it were a pipe.

And then he was before the table, before the face of the man he had never forgotten, whose memory had kept him alive the last ten years.

4

The voice had not deceived him; it was Karl Pfann. The German must have gained fifty pounds and he had lost nearly all his hair—only a few blond strands criss-crossed his greasy pate—but the mouth was as tiny and almost as cruel as Rogan remembered it. Rogan sat down at the next table and ordered a drink. When the house lights went out and the blue movie came on again he slipped the Walther pistol out of its holster and, keeping his hands under the table, fitted the silencer onto the pistol barrel. The weapon sagged out of balance; it would not be accurate beyond five yards. Rogan leaned to his right and tapped Karl Pfann on the shoulder.

The gross head turned, the shiny pate inclined, and the false-friendly voice Rogan had been hearing in his dreams for ten years said, "Yes, *mein Freund,* what do you wish?"

Rogan said in a hoarse voice, "I am an old comrade of yours. We made a business deal on *Rosenmontag,* Carnival Monday, 1945, in the Munich Palace of Justice."

The movie distracted Karl Pfann, and his eyes turned toward the bright screen. "No, no, it cannot be," he said impatiently. "In 1945 I was serving the Fatherland. I became a businessman after the war."

"When you were a Nazi," Rogan said. "When you were a torturer . . . When you were a murderer." The silver plate in his skull was throbbing. "My name is Michael Rogan. I was in American Intelligence. Do you remember me now?"

There was the smash of glass as Karl Pfann's huge body swiveled around and he peered through the darkness at Rogan. The German said quietly, menacingly, "Michael Rogan is dead. What do you want from me?"

5

"Your life," Rogan said. He swung the Walther pistol out from under the table and pressed it into Pfann's belly. He pulled the trigger. The German's body shuddered with the force of the bullet. Rogan reset the silencer and fired again. Pfann's choking death cry was drowned out by the roar of laughter sweeping through the nightclub as the screen showed a hilarious seduction scene.

Pfann's body slumped over the table. His murder would not be noticed until the movie ended. Rogan slipped the silencer off the pistol and put both pieces in his jacket pockets. He got up and moved silently through the darkened nightclub. The gold-braided doorman saluted him and whistled for a taxi, but Rogan turned his face away and walked down the Allee toward the waterfront. He walked along the waterfront for a long time, until his pulse slowed its wild galloping. In the cold north German moonlight, ruined U-boat pens and rust-covered submarines brought back the terrible ghosts of war.

Karl Pfann was dead. Two down and five to go, Rogan thought grimly. And then ten years of bad dreams would be paid for and he could make peace with the silver plate in his skull, the eternal screams of Christine calling his name, calling for salvation, and the blinding, flashing moment when seven men in a high-domed room of the Munich Palace of Justice had put him to death as if he were an animal. They had tried to murder him, without dignity, as a joke.

The wind along the waterfront cut into his body and Rogan turned up the Reeperbahn, Ropemaker's walk, passing the police station as he entered Davidstrasser. He was not afraid of the police. The light in the nightclub had been too dim for anyone to have seen him well enough to describe him accurately. Still, to be safe, he ducked into a side street that had a large wooden sign: "Adolescents Forbidden!" It seemed like any other street, until he turned the corner.

He had stumbled onto Hamburg's famous St. Pauli Alley, the city area set aside for legal prostitution. It was brilliantly lighted and thronged with strolling men. The gingerbread three-story houses seemed ordinary at first glance, except that parties were going on in all of them. The street-level floors had huge showcase windows, revealing the rooms within. Sitting in armchairs, reading, drinking coffee, and chatting, or lying on sofas and staring dreamily at the ceiling, were some of the most beautiful young girls Rogan had ever seen.

A few pretended to be cleaning their kitchens and wore only an apron that came to mid-thigh and had no back at all. Each house had a sign: "30 Marks for One Hour." On a few windows the shades were drawn. Printed in gold on the black shades was the word *Ausverkauft*, "Sold Out," to announce proudly that some well-to-do sport had hired the girl for the whole night.

There was one blonde who was reading at a zinc-topped table in her kitchen. She looked forlorn, never glancing up at the busy street; some coffee had spilled near her open book. Rogan stood outside the house and waited for her to raise her head so that he could see her face. But she would not look up. She must be ugly, Rogan thought. He would pay her thirty marks just so he could rest before he started the long walk back to his hotel. It was bad for him to get excited, the doctors had said, and

7

a woman with an ugly face would not excite him. With that silver plate in his skull Rogan was forbidden to drink hard liquor, make love excessively, or even become angry. They had not said anything to him about committing murder.

When he entered the brightly lighted kitchen he saw that the girl at the table was beautiful. She closed her book regretfully, got up, then took him by the hand and led him to the inner private room. Rogan felt a quick surge of desire that made his legs tremble, his head pound. The reaction of murder and flight hit him full force, and he felt himself becoming faint. He sank down on the bed, and the young girl's flutelike voice seemed to come from far away. "What's the matter with you? Are you ill?"

Rogan shook his head and fumbled with his wallet. He spread a sheaf of bills on the bed and said, "I am buying you for the night. Pull down your shade. Then just let me sleep." As she went back into the kitchen Rogan took a small bottle of pills from his shirt pocket and popped two of them into his mouth. It was the last thing he remembered doing before he lost consciousness.

When Rogan awoke the gray dawn smeared through dusty back windows to greet him. He looked around. The girl was sleeping on the floor beneath a thin blanket. A faint scent of roses came from her body. Rogan rolled over so that he could get out of the bed on the other side. The danger signals were gone. The silver plate no longer throbbed; the headache had vanished. He felt rested and strong.

Nothing had been taken from his wallet. The Walther

pistol was still in his jacket pocket. He had picked an honest girl who also had common sense, Rogan thought. He went around to the other side of the bed to wake her up, but she was already struggling to her feet, her beautiful body trembling in the morning cold.

The room smelled strongly of roses, Rogan noticed, and there were roses embroidered on the window curtains and on the bedsheets. There were even roses embroidered on the girl's sheer nightgown. She smiled at him. "My name is Rosalie. I like everything with roses— my perfumes, my clothing, everything."

She seemed girlishly proud of her fondness for roses, as if it gave her a special distinction. Rogan found this amusing. He sat on the bed and beckoned to her. Rosalie came and stood between his legs. He could smell her delicate perfume, and as she slowly took off her silk nightgown he could see the strawberry-tipped breasts, the long white thighs; and then her body was folding around his own like soft silky petals, and her full-lipped mouth bloomed open beneath his own, fluttering helplessly with passion.

CHAPTER 2

Rogan liked the girl so well that he arranged for her to live with him in his hotel for the next week. This involved complicated financial arrangements with the proprietor, but he didn't mind. Rosalie was delighted. Rogan got an almost paternal satisfaction out of her pleasure.

She was even more thrilled when she learned that his hotel was the world-famous Vier Jahrezeiten, the most luxurious hotel in postwar Hamburg, its service in the grand manner of the old Kaiser Germany.

Rogan treated Rosalie like a princess that week. He gave her money for new clothes, and he took her to the theater and to fine restaurants. She was an affectionate girl, but there was a strange blankness in her that puzzled Rogan. She responded to him as if he were something to love, just as a pet dog is something to love. She stroked his body as impersonally as she would stroke a fur coat, purring with the same kind of pleasure. One day she came back unexpectedly from a shopping trip and found Rogan cleaning his Walther P-38 pistol. That Rogan should own such a weapon was a matter of complete indifference to her. She really didn't care, and she didn't question him about it. Although Rogan was relieved that she reacted this way, he knew it wasn't natural.

Experience had taught Rogan that he needed a week's rest after one of his attacks. His next move was to Berlin, and toward the end of the week he debated whether or not to take Rosalie along to the divided city. He decided against it. Things might end badly, and she would be hurt through no fault of her own. On the last night he told her he would be leaving her in the morning and gave her all the cash in his wallet. With that strange blankness, she took the money and tossed it on the bed. She gave no sign of emotion other than a purely physical one of animal hunger. Because it was their last night together she wanted to make love for as long as possible. She began to take off her clothes. As she did so she asked casually, "Why must you go to Berlin?"

Rogan studied her creamy shoulders. "Business," he said.

"I looked in your special envelopes, all seven of them. I wanted to know more about you." She pulled off her stockings. "The night you met me you killed Karl Pfann, and his envelope and photograph are marked with the number two. The envelope and picture of Albert Moltke are marked 'number one,' so I went to the library and found the Vienna newspapers. Moltke was killed a month ago. Your passport shows you were in Austria at that time. Envelopes three and four are marked with the names of Eric and Hans Freisling, and they live in Berlin. So you are going to Berlin to kill them when you leave me tomorrow. And you plan to kill the other three men also, numbers five, six, and seven. Isn't that true?"

Rosalie spoke matter-of-factly, as if his plans were not extraordinary in any way. Naked, she sat on the edge of the bed, waiting for him to make love to her. For a bizarre moment Rogan thought of killing her and rejected it; and then he realized that it would not be necessary. She would never betray him. There was that curious blankness in her eyes, as if she had no capacity to distinguish between good and evil.

He knelt before her on the bed and bent his head between her breasts. He took her hand in his, and it was warm and dry; she was not afraid. He guided her hand to the back of his skull, made her run her fingers over the silver plate. It was concealed by hair brushed over it, and part of it was overgrown with a thin membrane of dead, horny skin; but he knew she could feel the metal. "Those seven men did that to me," he said. "It keeps me alive, but I'll never see any grandchildren. I'll never live to be an old man sitting in the sun."

Her fingers touched the back of his skull, not recoiling from the metal or the horny, dead flesh. "I'll help you if you want me to," she said; and he could smell the scent of roses on her and he thought, knowing it was sentimental, that roses were for weddings, not for death.

"No," he said. "I'll leave tomorrow. Forget about me. Forget you ever saw those envelopes. OK?"

"OK," Rosalie said, "I'll forget about you." She paused, and for a moment that curious emptiness left her and she asked, "Will you forget about me?"

"No," Rogan said.

CHAPTER 3

M ike Rogan never forgot a thing. At the age of five he told his mother in detail what had happened to him three years earlier when, at the age of two, he'd been seriously ill with pneumonia. He told her the name of the hospital, which his mother no longer remembered; he described the hospital pediatrician, an extraordinarily ugly man who had a marvelous way with children. The pediatrician would even let youngsters play with the star-shaped disfiguring wen on his chin so that they would not be afraid of it. Michael Rogan remembered trying to pull the wen off and the pediatrician letting out a comical "ouch!"

His mother was astounded by and a little fearful of Michael's memory feat, but his father was overjoyed. Joseph Rogan was a hardworking accountant, and he had visions of his son becoming a CPA before he was twenty-one and earning a good living. His thoughts went no further, until little Michael Rogan came home from kindergarten with a note from his teacher. The note informed the Rogans that parents and son should appear at the school principal's office the next day to discuss Michael's academic future.

The interview was short and to the point. Michael could not be permitted to attend kindergarten with the rest of the children. He was a disruptive influence. He corrected the teacher when she left some little detail out of a story. He already knew how to read and write. He would have to be sent to a special school, or take his chances in the higher grades immediately. His parents decided to send him to a special school.

At the age of nine, when the other boys were running into the street with baseball gloves or footballs, Michael Rogan would leave his house carrying a genuine leather briefcase that had his initials and address stamped on it in gold. Inside the briefcase was the text of whatever subject he was studying that particular week. It rarely took him more than a week to master a subject that normally required a year's study. He would simply memorize all the texts by reading them once. And it was only natural that such a boy was considered a freak in his neighborhood.

One day a group of kids his own age surrounded Michael Rogan. One of them, a chunky blond boy, said to him, "Don't you ever play?" Rogan didn't answer. The blond boy said, "You can play on my side. We're gonna play football."

"All right," Michael said. "I'll play."

That day was a glorious day for him. He found out that he had good physical coordination and that he could hold his own playing football or fighting with other boys. He came home for supper with his expensive leather briefcase smeared with mud. He also had a black eye and puffy, bloody lips. But he was so proud and so happy that he ran to his mother shouting, "I'm going to be on the football team! They picked me to be on the football team!"

Alice Rogan took one look at his battered face and burst into tears.

She tried to be reasonable. She explained to her young son that his brain was valuable, that he should never expose it to any danger. "You have an extraordinary mind, Michael," she said. "Your mind may someday help humanity. You can't be like other boys. What if you should hurt your head playing football? Or fighting with another boy?"

Michael listened and understood. When his father came home that evening he said almost the same thing. So Michael gave up all thoughts of being like ordinary boys. He had a precious treasure to guard for humanity. Had he been older he would have realized that his parents were being pompous and a bit ridiculous about this treasure, but he had not yet acquired that kind of adult judgment.

When he was thirteen the other boys started to humiliate him, taunt him, knock his briefcase from his hands. Michael Rogan, obeying his parents, refused to fight and suffered humiliation. It was his father who began to have doubts about how his son was being brought up.

One day Joseph Rogan brought home huge, puffy

boxing gloves and taught his son the art of self-defense. Joseph told him to stick up for himself, to fight if necessary. "It's more important that you grow up to be a man," he said, "than to be a genius."

It was during his thirteenth year that Michael Rogan discovered he was different from ordinary boys in another way. His parents had always taught him to dress neatly and in an adult fashion, because he spent so much of his time studying with adults. One day a group of boys surrounded Rogan and told him they were going to take off his pants and hang them from a lamppost, a routine humiliation most of the boys had undergone.

Rogan went berserk when they put their hands on him. He sank his teeth into one boy's ear and ripped it partly from the boy's head. He got his hand around the ringleader's throat and throttled him, despite other boys kicking and punching him to make him let go. When some grown-ups finally broke up the fight, three of the group and Rogan had to be hospitalized.

But nobody ever bothered him again. He was shunned not only as a freak but as a violent freak.

Michael Rogan was intelligent enough to know that his rage was not natural, that it sprang from some deeper source. And he came to understand what it was. He was enjoying the fruits of his extraordinary memory, his intellectual powers, without having done anything to deserve them, and he felt guilty about it. He talked of his feelings with his father, who understood and started to make plans for Michael to lead a more normal life. Unhappily, Joseph Rogan died of a heart attack before he could help his son.

Michael Rogan, going on fifteen, was tall, strong, and well coordinated. He was absorbing knowledge on the advanced levels now; and under the complete dominance of his mother, he really believed that his mind was a sacred trust to be guarded for its future use to humanity. By this time he had his MA and was studying for his MS. His mother treated him like a reigning king. That year Michael Rogan discovered girls.

In this he was perfectly normal. But he discovered to his chagrin that girls were afraid of him and treated him with giggling teenage cruelty. He was so intellectually mature that once again he was regarded as a freak by those his age. This drove him back to his studies with renewed fury.

At eighteen he found himself accepted as an equal by the seniors and graduate students at the Ivy League school where he was completing studies for his PhD in mathematics. The girls, too, seemed to be attracted to him now. Big for his age, he was broad through the shoulders, and could easily pass for twenty-two or twenty-three. He learned to disguise his brilliance so that it would not be too frightening, and at last he got into bed with a girl.

Marian Hawkins was a blonde who was dedicated to her studies, but she was also dedicated to all-night parties. She was his steady sex partner for a year. Rogan neglected his studies, drank a great deal of beer, and committed all the natural stupidities of a normal growing boy. His mother was distressed at this turn of events, but Rogan did not let her distress bother him at all. Though he would never admit it to himself, he disliked his mother.

The Japanese attacked Pearl Harbor on the day Rogan was assured of his doctorate. By now Rogan had tired of Marian Hawkins and was looking for a graceful way out. He was tired of training his mind and tired also of his mother. He was hungry for excitement and adventure. On the day after Pearl Harbor he sat down and wrote a long letter to the chief of Army Intelligence. He made a list of his academic awards and achievements and enclosed them with the letter. Less than a week later he received a telegram from Washington, asking him to report for an interview.

The interview was one of the bright moments of his life. He was interrogated by a crew-cut Intelligence captain who looked over the list Rogan had sent with a bored expression. He seemed unimpressed, especially when he learned that Rogan had no background of athletic activity.

Captain Alexander pushed Rogan's papers back into a manila folder and took it into the inner office. He was gone for a while, and when he came back he had a mimeographed sheet in his hand. He put it on the desk in front of him and tapped it with his pencil. "This sheet is covered with a coded message. It's an old, outdated code we no longer use. But I want to see if you can figure it out. Don't be surprised if you find it too difficult; after all you've had no training." He handed the sheet to Rogan.

Rogan looked it over. It appeared to be a standard cryptographic letter substitution, relatively simple. Rogan had studied cryptography and the theory of codes when he was eleven years old, for mental kicks. He picked up a pencil and got to work, and in five minutes he read the translated message to Captain Alexander.

The captain disappeared into the other room and returned with a manila folder from which he took a sheet of paper containing only two paragraphs. This was a more difficult code, and its brevity made it that much harder to decode. It took Rogan almost an hour to break it. Captain Alexander looked at his translation and disappeared again into the inner office. The next time he came out he was accompanied by a gray-haired colonel, who sat in a corner of the reception room and studied Rogan intently.

Now Captain Alexander handed Rogan three sheets of paper covered with symbols. He smiled a little this time. Rogan recognized that smile; he had seen it on the faces of teachers and specialists who thought they had Rogan in a spot. So he was very careful with the code, and it took him three hours to break it. He was so concentrated on his task that he didn't notice the room filling up with officers, all watching him intently. When Rogan finished he handed his yellow work sheets to the captain. Captain Alexander scanned the translation swiftly and without a word handed it to the gray-haired colonel. The colonel ran his eyes down the paper and then said curtly to the captain, "Bring him to my office."

To Rogan, the whole thing had been an enjoyable exercise, and he was startled to see the colonel looked worried. The first thing he said to Rogan was, "You've made this a bad day for me, young man."

"I'm sorry," Rogan said politely. He didn't really give a damn. Captain Alexander had irritated him.

"It's not your fault," the colonel growled. "None of us thought you could break that last code. It's one of our best, and now that you know it we'll have to change over. After we screen you and accept you in the services maybe we can use the code again."

Rogan said incredulously, "You mean all the codes are that easy?"

The colonel said drily, "To you they are, obviously. To anybody else they are all that hard. Are you prepared to enter the service immediately?"

Rogan nodded. "This very minute."

The colonel frowned. "It doesn't work that way. You have to be screened for security. And until you are cleared, we'll have to keep you under arrest. You already know too much to be running around loose. But that's just a formality."

The formality proved to be an Intelligence department prison that made Alcatraz seem like a summer camp. But it did not occur to Rogan that this treatment was typical of all Intelligence attitudes. A week later he was sworn into the service as a second lieutenant. Three months later he was in charge of the section responsible for breaking all European codes, except for Russia's. The Russian code was part of the Asian section.

He was happy. For the first time in his life he was doing something dramatic and exciting. His memory, his fabulously brilliant mind, was helping his country to win a great war. He had his pick of young girls in Washington. And soon he was promoted. Life couldn't be better. But in 1943 he had begun to feel guilty again. He felt that he was using his mental ability to avoid front-line action, and he volunteered for the field intelligence section. His offer was rejected; he was too valuable to be risked.

It was then that he came up with the idea of himself as a walking code switchboard to coordinate the invasion of France from inside that country. He prepared the plan in detail; it was brilliant, and the chiefs of staff approved. And so the brilliant Captain Rogan was parachuted into France.

He was proud of himself, and he knew that his father, too, would have been proud of what he was doing now. But his mother wept because he was endangering his brain, that fabulous brain they had sheltered and nurtured for so long. Rogan shrugged it off. He hadn't yet done anything so marvelous with his brain. Perhaps after the war he would find his real interest and establish his true genius. But he had learned enough to know that raw brilliance needs long years of hard work to develop properly. He would have time after the war. On New Year's Day, 1944, Captain Michael Rogan was parachuted into Occupied France as chief Allied communications officer with the French Underground. He had trained with Britain's SOE Agents, had learned how to operate a secret radio transmitter-receiver, and was carrying a tiny suicide capsule surgically embedded in the palm of his left hand.

His billet hideout was in the house of a French family named Charney in the town of Vitry-sur-Seine, just south of Paris. There Rogan set up his network of couriers and informers and radioed coded information to England. On occasion he received radioed requests for certain details needed for the coming invasion of Europe.

It proved to be a quiet, peaceful life. On fine Sunday afternoons he went on picnics with the daughter of the house, Christine Charney, a long-limbed, sweet-looking girl with chestnut hair. Christine studied music at the local university. She and Michael Rogan became lovers, and then she became pregnant.

Wearing his beret and flashing his false ID papers, Rogan married Christine Charney at the town hall and they returned to her parents' house to carry out the work of the Underground together.

When the Allies invaded Normandy on June 6, 1944, Rogan had so much communication traffic on his radio that he became careless. Two weeks later the Gestapo swooped down on the Charney house and arrested everyone inside it. They waited for exactly the right moment. Not only did they arrest the Charney family and Mike Rogan; they also arrested six Underground couriers waiting for messages. Within a month all were interrogated, tried, and executed. All except Michael Rogan and his wife, Christine. From the interrogation of the other prisoners the Germans had learned about Rogan's ability to memorize intricate codes, and they wanted to give him special attention. His wife was kept alive, Rogan was smilingly told, "as a special courtesy." She was then five months pregnant.

Six weeks after their capture, Michael Rogan and his wife were put in separate Gestapo staff cars and driven to Munich. In that city's busy central square stood the Munich Palace of Justice, and in one of those court buildings, Michael Rogan's final and most terrible interrogation began. It lasted for endless days, more days than he could count. But in the years afterward his fabulous memory spared him nothing. It repeated his agony second by second, over and over again. He suffered a thousand separate nightmares. And it always began with the seven-man interrogation team waiting for him in the high-domed room of the Munich Palace of Justice—waiting patiently and with good humor, for the sport that would give them pleasure.

All seven wore swastika armbands, but two men wore tunics of different shades. From this and the collar insignia, Rogan knew that one of them was with the Hungarian armed forces and the other was with the Italian army. These two took no part in the interrogation at first; they were official observers.

The chief of the interrogation team was a tall, aristocratic officer with deep-set eyes. He assured Rogan that all they wanted was the codes stored in his head, and then Rogan and his wife and the unborn child would live. They hammered at him all that first day, and Rogan stood mute. He refused to answer any questions. Then on the night of the second day he heard Christine's voice screaming for help in the next room. She kept calling his name, screaming, "Michel! Michel!" over and over. She was in agony. Rogan looked at the burning eyes of the chief interrogator and whispered, "Stop that. Stop. I'll tell you everything."

For the next five days he gave them old, discarded code combinations. In some way, perhaps by comparing them with intercepted messages, they learned what he was doing. The next day they seated him in the chair and stood around in a circle. They did not question him; they did not touch him. The man in the Italian uniform disappeared into the other room. A few moments later Rogan heard his wife screaming in agony again. The pain in her voice was beyond belief. Rogan started to whisper that he would tell them everything, anything they wanted to know, but the chief interrogator shook his head. They all sat in silence as the screams pierced the walls and their brains, until Rogan slipped from his chair to the floor, weeping, almost unconscious with grief. Then they dragged him across the floor of the high-domed room and into the next chamber. The interrogator in the Italian uniform was sitting beside a phonograph. The twirling black record sent Christine's screams shrieking through the Palace of Justice.

"You never tricked us," the chief interrogator said contemptuously. "We outwitted you. Your wife died under torture the very first day." Rogan studied their faces carefully. If they let him live, he would kill them all someday.

He realized only later that this was exactly the reaction they wanted. They promised to let him live if he would give them the correct codes. And in his desire for vengeance, he did so. For the next two weeks he gave them the codes and explained how they worked. He was sent back to his solitary cell for what seemed many more months. Once a week he would be escorted to the high-domed room and interrogated by the seven men in what he came to realize was a purely routine procedure. There was no way for Rogan to know that during these months the Allied armies had swept across France and into Germany and were now at the gates of Munich. When he was summoned for his final interrogation he could not know that the seven interrogators were about to flee and disguise their identities, disappear into the mass of Germans in a desperate effort to escape punishment for their crimes.

"We are going to set you free; we are going to keep our promise," the aristocratic chief interrogator with the deep-set eyes said to Rogan. That voice rang with sincerity. It was an actor's voice, or an orator's. One of the other men pointed to some civilian clothes lying over the back of a chair. "Take off your rags and change into these."

Unbelieving, Rogan changed his clothes before their eyes. There was even a wide-brimmed fedora, which one of the men jammed on his head. They all grinned at him in a friendly way. The aristocratic officer said in his sincere, bell-toned voice, "Isn't it good to know that you will be free? That you will live?"

But suddenly Rogan knew he was lying. There was something wrong. Only six men were in the room with him, and they were smiling secret, evil smiles. At that moment Rogan felt the cold metal of the gun touch the back of his head. His hat tilted forward as the gun barrel pushed up against its brim, and Rogan felt the sickening terror of a man about to be killed. It was all a cruel charade and they were killing him as they would kill an animal, as a joke. And then a great roar filled his brain, as if he had fallen under water, and his body was torn out of the space it filled, exploded into a black, endless void. . . .

That Rogan lived was a miracle. He had been shot in the back of the head, and his body was thrown on a pile of corpses, other prisoners executed in the courtyard of the Munich Palace of Justice. Six hours later, advance elements of the U.S. Third Army entered Munich, and its medical units found the great pile of bodies. When they came to Rogan they found him still alive. The bullet had deflected off the skull bone, tearing a hole in, but not penetrating, the brain—a type of wound not uncommon with shell fragments but rarely made by small arms.

Rogan was operated on in a forward field hospital and sent back to the United States. He spent another two years in various army hospitals for special treatment. The wound had impaired his sight; he could see only straight ahead, with very little lateral vision. With training, his vision improved enough for him to get a driver's license and live an ordinary life. But he had come to rely on his hearing more than his sight, whenever possible. At the end of the two years the silver plate put in his skull to hold the shattered bones together seemed a natural part of him. Except in moments of stress. Then it felt as if all the blood in his brain pounded against it.

When he was released the doctors told Rogan that drinking liquor would be bad for him, that sexual intercourse to excess would do him harm, that it would be better if he did not smoke. He was assured that his intellectual capacities had not been damaged, but that he would need more rest than the average man. He was also given medication for the intermittent headaches. Internal cranial pressure would build up as a result of the damaged condition of his skull and the silver plate.

In brief, his brain was terribly vulnerable to any kind of physical or emotional stress. With care he could live to be fifty, even sixty. He was to follow instructions, take his medication regularly—which included tranquilizers—and report to a VA hospital every month for check-ups and changes in medication. His fabulous memory, Rogan was assured, was not impaired in the slightest. And that had proved to be the final irony.

In the ten years that followed, he obeyed instructions, he took his medication, he reported to the VA hospital every month. But what finally proved his undoing was his magic memory. At night when he went to bed it was as if a movie unreeled before his eyes. He saw the seven men in the high-domed room of the Munich Palace of Justice in minute detail. He felt his hat brim tilt forward, the gun cold against his neck. The black roaring void swallowed him up. And when he closed his eyes he heard Christine's terrible screams from the next room.

The ten years were a continuous nightmare. When he was released from the hospital he decided to make his home in New York City. His mother had died after he had been reported missing in action, so there was no sense in returning to his home town. And he thought that in New York he might find the proper use for his abilities.

He got a job with one of the mammoth insurance companies. The work was one of simple statistical analysis, but to his amazement he found it was beyond him; he could not concentrate. He was discharged for incompetence, a humiliation that set him back physically as well as mentally. It also increased his distrust of his fellow human beings. Where the hell did they come off, firing him after he had had his head blown apart protecting their skins during the war?

He took a job as a government clerk in the Veterans Administration building in New York. He was given a

GS-3 grade, which paid him sixty dollars a week, and asked to do only the simplest of tasks in filing and sorting. Millions of new files were being set up on the new veterans of World War II, and it was this that started him thinking about computers. But it was to be two years later before his brain could really work out the complicated mathematical formulae that such computer systems needed.

He lived a drab existence in the great city. His $60 a week was barely enough to cover necessary expenses, such as the little efficiency apartment on the outskirts of Greenwich Village, frozen foods, and whiskey. He needed the whiskey to get drunk enough so that he would not dream when he slept.

Spending every working day filing dreary documents, he would come home to the shabby apartment and cook frozen foods to warm, tasteless pulp. Then he would drink half of a bottle of whiskey and sink into a sodden slumber on his rumpled bed, sometimes without taking his clothes off. And still the nightmares came. But the nightmares were not much worse than the reality had been.

In the Munich Palace of Justice they had stripped him of his dignity. They had done what the boys had threatened to do to him when he was thirteen years old, the harsh adult equivalent of taking off his trousers and hanging them on the lamppost. They had mixed laxatives with this food and that, along with the fear and the thin gruel that was called oatmeal at breakfast and stew at night, made his bowels uncontrollable; the food ran through him. When he was dragged out of his cell for the daily interrogation at the long table he could feel the seat of his pants sticky against his buttocks. He could smell the stench. But worse, he could see the cruel grins on the faces of his interrogators, and he would feel ashamed as a little boy feels ashamed. And yet in some way it made him feel closer to the seven men who were torturing him.

Now, years later, alone in his apartment, he would relive the physical indignities. He was shy and would not go out of the apartment to meet people, nor would he accept invitations to parties. He met a girl who worked as a clerk in the VA building, and with a tremendous effort of will made himself respond to her obvious interest. She came to his apartment for a drink and dinner and made it plain that she was willing to stay the night. But when Rogan went to bed with her, he was impotent.

It was a few weeks after this that his supervisor called him into the personnel office. The supervisor was a World War II veteran who thought that his job of supervising thirty file clerks proved he was mentally superior to the men under him. Trying to be kind to Rogan, he said, "Maybe this work is just a little too hard for you right now; maybe you should do some kind of physical work, like running the elevator. You know what I mean?"

The very fact that it was well intentioned made it more galling to Rogan. As a disabled veteran he had a right to appeal his discharge. The personnel officer at the conference advised him not to do so. "We can prove that you're just not bright enough to do this job," he told Rogan. "We have your Civil Service exam marks, and they just barely qualify you. So I think you'd be wise to take the medical discharge from government service. Then maybe if you go to night school you can do a little better."

Rogan was so astonished that he burst out laughing. He reasoned that part of his file must be missing, or that these people thought he had filled out his forms falsely. That was it, he thought, as he saw them smiling at him. They thought he had faked everything in his educational files. Rogan laughed again and walked out of the personnel office, out of the building, out of the insultingly drab job that he could not even perform properly. He never went back, and one month later he received his employment discharge in the post. He was reduced to living on his disability pension, which he had previously never touched.

With more time on his hands, he drank more. He took a room near the Bowery and became one of the countless derelicts who spent the day drinking cheap wine until they became unconscious. Two months later he was back in the Veterans Administration as a patient. But not for his head wound. He was suffering from malnutrition and so dangerously debilitated that a common cold might finish him off.

It was while he was in the hospital that he ran into one of his childhood friends, Philip Houke, who was being treated for an ulcer. It was Houke, now a lawyer, who got Rogan his first job with computers. It was Houke who brought Rogan into some contact with humanity again, by reminding him of his former brilliance.

But it was a long, hard road coming back. Rogan stayed in the hospital for six months, the first three to "dry out." The final three months he underwent new tests on his skull injury, plus special mental-fatigue tests. For the first time a complete and correct diagnosis was made: Michael Rogan's brain retained its almost super-human memory capacity and some of its creative brilliance. But it could not stand up to long uninterrupted use or extended stress without blurring with fatigue. He would never be able to put in the long hard hours of concentration that creative research demanded. Even simple tasks requiring long consecutive hours of work were now out of the question.

Instead of this news dismaying him, Michael Rogan was pleased that finally he knew exactly where he stood. He was also relieved of his guilt, for he was no longer responsible for a "treasure to humanity." When Philip Houke arranged for him to work with one of the new computer firms, Rogan found that unconsciously his mind had been working on computer construction problems ever since he had been a file clerk for the VA. So in less than a year he solved many of the technical construction problems with his knowledge of math. Houke demanded a partnership in the firm for Rogan, and became his financial advisor. In the next few years Rogan's computer firm became one of the top ten in the country. Then it went public, and its shares tripled in value within a year. Rogan became known as the genius in the field, and was asked to advise on administrative procedures when the separate service departments were consolidated into the Defense Department. He also became a millionaire. Ten years after the war he was a success, despite the fact that he could not work more than an hour a day.

Philip Houke took care of all his business affairs and

became his best friend. Houke's wife tried to get Rogan interested in her unmarried girlfriends, but none of the affairs ever became serious. His fabulous memory still worked against him. On bad nights he still heard Christine screaming in the Munich Palace of Justice. And he felt again the wet stickiness on his buttocks as the seven interrogators watched him with their contemptuous grins. He could never start a new life, he thought, not with another woman.

During those years Rogan kept track of every trial of war criminals in postwar Germany. He subscribed to a European newspaper clipping service, and when he started to collect patent royalties he retained a German private detective agency in Berlin to send him photographs of all accused war criminals no matter how low their rank. It seemed a hopeless task to find seven men whose names he did not know and who were surely making every effort to stay hidden among Europe's millions.

His first break came when the private detective agency sent him a photograph of a dignified-looking Austrian city official, with the caption "Albert Moltke acquitted. Retains electoral position despite former Nazi ties." The face was the face of one of the seven men he sought.

Rogan had never forgiven himself for his carelessness in transmitting radio messages on D-day, the carelessness that had led to the discovery and the destruction of his Underground group. But he had learned from it. Now he proceeded cautiously and with the utmost precision. He increased his retainer to the detective firm in Germany and instructed them to keep Albert Moltke under close surveillance for a year. At the end of that time he had three more photographs, with names and addresses, three more dossiers of the men who had murdered his wife and tortured him in the Munich Palace of Justice. One was Karl Pfann, in the export-import business in Hamburg. The other two were brothers, Eric and Hans Freisling, who owned a mechanic's shop and gas station in West Berlin. Rogan decided that the time had come.

He made his preparations very carefully. He had his company appoint him as its European sales representative, with letters of introduction to computer firms in Germany and Austria. He had no fear of being recognized. His terrible wound and his years of suffering had changed his appearance a great deal; and besides, he was a dead man. So far as his interrogators knew, they had killed Captain Michael Rogan.

Rogan took a plane to Vienna and set up his business headquarters there. He checked into the Sacher Hotel, had a fine dinner, with the renowned *Sachertorte* for dessert, and sipped brandy in the hotel's famous Red Bar. Later he took a walk through the twilit streets, listening to the zither music emanating from the cafés. He walked for a long time, until he was relaxed enough to return to his room and sleep.

During the next two weeks, through friendly Austrians he met at two computer firms, Rogan got himself invited to the important parties in Vienna. Finally, at a municipal ball, which the city bureaucrats had to attend, he met Albert Moltke. He was surprised that the man had changed so much. The face had mellowed with good living and good food. The hair was silver gray. The whole attitude of his body suggested the politician's surface politeness. And on his arm was his wife, a slender, cheerful-looking woman, obviously much younger than he was and obviously much in love with him. When he noticed Rogan staring at him, Moltke bowed politely, as if to say, "Yes, thank you for voting for me. I remember you very well, of course. Come and see me any time in my office." It was the bow of an expert politician. No wonder he beat the rap when he'd been tried as a war criminal, Rogan thought. And he took some pleasure in knowing that it was the acquittal and the resultant photograph in the newspapers that had sentenced Albert Moltke to death.

Albert Moltke had bowed to the stranger, though his feet were killing him and he was wishing with all his heart that he was back home beside his own fireplace drinking black coffee and eating *Sachertorte*. These fêtes were a bore, but after all the *Partei* had to raise election funds somehow. And he owed it to his colleagues after they had supported him so loyally during the late troubled times. Moltke felt his wife, Ursula, press his arm, and he bowed again to the stranger, feeling vaguely that it was someone important, someone he should remember more clearly.

Yes, the *Partei* and his dear Ursula had rallied around when he had been accused as a war criminal. And after he had been acquitted the trial turned out to be his best piece of luck. He had won election to one of the local councils, and his political future, though limited, was assured. It would be a good living. But then the disturbing thought came as it always came: What if the *Partei* and

Ursula found out the charges were true? Would his wife still love him? Would she leave him if she knew the truth? No, she could never believe him capable of such crimes, no matter what the proof. He could hardly believe it himself. He had been a different man then—harder, colder, stronger. In those times one had to be like that to survive. And yet . . . and yet . . . how could it be? When he tucked his two young children in bed his hands sometimes hesitated in the act of touching them. Such hands could not touch such innocence. But the jury had freed him. They had acquitted him after weighing all the evidence, and he could not be tried again. He, Albert Moltke, was forever innocent, according to law. And yet . . . and yet . . .

The stranger was coming toward him. A tall, powerfully built man, with an oddly shaped head. Handsome, in a dark German way. But then Albert Moltke noticed the well-tailored suit. No, this man was an American, obviously. Moltke had met many of them since the war, in the transaction of business. He smiled his welcome and turned to introduce his wife, but she had wandered off a few steps and was talking to someone else. And then the American was introducing himself. His name sounded something like Rogan and this, too, was vaguely familiar to Moltke. "Congratulations on your promotion to the *Recordat*. And congratulations on your acquittal some time ago."

Moltke gave him a polite smile. He recited his standard speech. "A patriotic jury did its duty and decided, fortunately for me, for an innocent fellow German."

They chatted awhile. The American suggested that he could use some legal help on setting up his computer business. Moltke became interested. He knew that the American really meant he wanted to bypass a few city taxes. Moltke, knowing from past experience that this could make him rich, took the American by the arm and said, "Why don't we get a little bit of fresh air, take a little stroll?" The American smiled and nodded. Moltke's wife did not see them leave.

As they walked through the city streets the American asked casually, "Don't you remember my face?"

Moltke grimaced and said, "My dear sir, you do seem familiar, but I meet a lot of people, after all." He was a little impatient; he wished the American would get down to business.

With a slight sense of uneasiness, Moltke realized that now they were walking in a deserted alley. Then the American leaned close to Moltke's ear and whispered something that almost made his heart stop beating: "Do you remember *Rosenmontag*, 1945? In Munich? In the Palace of Justice?"

And then Moltke remembered the face; and he was not surprised when the American said, "My name is Rogan." With the fear that flooded through him there was overwhelming shame, as if for the first time he truly believed in his own guilt.

Rogan saw the recognition in Moltke's eyes. He steered the little man deeper into the alley, feeling Moltke's body trembling, trembling under his arm. "I won't hurt you," he said. "I only want some information about the other men, your comrades. I know Karl Pfann and the Freisling brothers. What were the names of the other three men, and where can I find them?"

Moltke was terrified. He started running clumsily down the alley. Rogan ran beside him, sprinting easily, as if the two of them were trotting together for exercise. Coming up on the Austrian's left side, Rogan drew the Walther pistol from his shoulder holster. Still running, he fitted the silencer onto the barrel. He felt no pity; he considered no mercy. Moltke's sins were etched in his brain, committed a thousand times in his memory. It had been Moltke who had smiled when Christine screamed in the next room, and who had murmured, "Come, don't be so much a hero at your poor wife's expense. Don't you want your child to be born?" So reasonable, so persuasive, when he knew that Christine was already dead. Moltke was the least of them but the memories of him had to die. Rogan fired two shots into Moltke's side. Moltke swooped forward in a falling glide; and Rogan kept running, out of the alley and onto a main street. The next day he took a plane to Hamburg.

In Hamburg it had been easy to track down Karl Pfann. Pfann had been the most brutal of the interrogators, but in such an animallike way that Rogan had despised him less than the others. Pfann had acted according to his true nature. He was a simple man, stupid and cruel. Rogan had killed him with less hatred than he had killed Moltke. It had gone exactly according to plan. What had not gone according to plan was Rogan's meeting the German girl Rosalie, with her flower fragrance and her curious lack of emotion and her amoral innocence.

Now lying beside her in his Hamburg hotel room, Rogan ran his hands lightly over her body. He had told her everything, sure that she would not betray him—or perhaps in the hope that she would, and so end his murdering quest. "Still like me?" he asked.

Rosalie nodded. She held his hand to her breast. "Let me help you," she said. "I don't care about anyone. I don't care if they die. But I care about you—a little bit. Take me to Berlin and I'll do anything you want me to."

Rogan knew she meant every word. He looked into her eyes and was troubled by the childlike innocence he saw there, and the emotional blankness, as if murdering and making love were, to her, equally permissible.

He decided to take her along. He liked having her around, and she would be a real help. Besides, there didn't seem to be anything or anyone else she cared about. And he would never involve her in the actual executions.

The next day he took her shopping on the Esplanade and in the arcade of the Baseler Hospitz. He bought her two new outfits that set off the pale rose skin, the blue of her eyes. They went back to the hotel and packed, and after supper they caught the night flight to Berlin.

CHAPTER 4

everal months after the war ended, Rogan had been
flown from his VA hospital in the United States to
U.S. Intelligence headquarters in Berlin. There he had
been asked to look at a number of suspected war criminals to see if any of them were men who had tortured
him in the Munich Palace of Justice. His case was now
file number A23,486 in the archives of the Allied War
Crimes Commission. Among the suspects were none of
the men he remembered so clearly. He could not identify
a single one, so he was flown back to the VA hospital. But
he had spent a few days wandering around the city, the
rubble of countless homes giving him a measure of sav-
age satisfaction.

The great city had changed in the years since then.
The West Berlin authorities had given up trying to clear
away the seventy million tons of ruins which the Allied
bombers had created during the war. They had pushed
the rubble into small artificial hills, then had planted

flowers and small shrubs over them. They had used the rubble to fill foundations for towering new apartment houses, built in the most modern space-conserving style. Berlin was now a huge steel gray rat warren of stone, and at night that warren showed the most vicious nests of vice spawned by ravaged postwar Europe.

With Rosalie, Rogan checked into the Kempinski Hotel on the Kurfürstendamm and Fasanenstrasse, perhaps the most elegant hotel in West Germany. Then he made a few telephone calls to some of the firms with which his company did business, and he set up an appointment with the private detective agency that had been on his payroll for the past five years.

For their first lunch together in Berlin, he took Rosalie to a restaurant called the Ritz that served the finest Oriental food. He noticed with amusement that Rosalie ate a huge amount of food with huge enjoyment. They ordered bird's nest soup, which looked like a tangle of vegetable brains stained with black blood. Her favorite dish was a combination of red lobster pieces, white pork chunks, and brown shards of nutmegged beef, but she found the barbecued spare ribs and the chicken with tender snow peas delicious. She sampled his shrimp with black bean sauce and nodded her approval. All of it was accompanied by several helpings of fried rice and innumerable cups of hot tea. It was an enormous lunch, but Rosalie put it away without any effort. She had just discovered that there was other food in the world besides bread, meat, and potatoes. Rogan, smiling at her pleasure, watched her finish off what was left on the silver-covered platters.

In the afternoon they went shopping along the Kur-fürstendamm, whose brightly lit store windows trailed off into gray, empty storefronts as the boulevard approached the Berlin Wall. Rogan bought Rosalie an expensive gold wristwatch with a clever roof of precious stones that slid back when its owner wanted to know the time. Rosalie squealed with delight, and Rogan thought wryly that if the way to a man's heart was through his stomach, then the way to a woman's heart was paved with gifts. But when she leaned over to kiss him, when he felt her soft, fluttering mouth on his own, his cynicism vanished.

That evening he took her to the Eldorado Club, where the waiters dressed as girls and the girls dressed as men. Then on to the Cherchelle Femme, where pretty girls on the stage stripped as casually as if they were in their own private bedrooms, with intimate wriggles and vulgar scratches. Finally the girls danced before huge mirrors wearing only long black hose and saucy red caps on their heads. Rogan and Rosalie ended up at the Badewanne in Nürnburg Strasse. They drank champagne and ate small, thick white sausages from large platters, using their fingers and wiping their hands on the tablecloth, like everyone else.

By the time they got back to their hotel suite Rogan was almost sick with sexual desire. He wanted to make love immediately, but Rosalie, laughing, pushed him away and disappeared into the bedroom. Frustrated, Rogan took off his jacket and tie and started to mix a drink at the little bar that was part of every suite. In a few minutes he heard Rosalie call, "Michael," in her soft, almost adolescent-sweet voice. He turned toward her.

49

On her blond head was a new hat he had bought her in Hamburg, a lovely creation of green ribbon. On her legs were long black net stockings that reached almost to the tops of her thighs. Between the green hat and black stockings was Rosalie—in the flesh. She came toward him slowly, smiling that intently happy smile of a woman roused to passion.

Rogan reached for her. She eluded his grasp, and he followed her into the bedroom, hastily pulling off the rest of his clothes on the way. When he reached for her this time, she did not move away. And then they were on the king-size bed, and he could smell the rose fragrance of her body, feel the petal-velvet skin as together they sank into an act of love that blotted out the hoarse night noises of Berlin, the plaintive cries of the animals imprisoned in the Tiergarten just below their windows, and the ghostly images of murder and revenge that haunted Rogan's vulnerable brain.

CHAPTER 5

Rogan wanted his first contact with the Freisling brothers to be casual. The next day he rented a Mercedes, drove it to the brothers' gas station, and had the car checked. He was attended to by Hans Freisling, and when Rogan went to the office to pay his bill, Eric was there, in a leather chair, checking oil-storage accounts.

The brothers had both aged well, perhaps because they had been unattractive to begin with. Age had tightened their loose, sly mouths; their lips were not so thick. They had become smarter in their dress and less vulgar in their speech. But they had not changed in their treachery, though it was now petty larceny instead of murder.

The Mercedes had been checked out that day by the rental agency and was in perfect condition. But Hans Freisling was charging him twenty marks for some minor mechanical adjustments and telling him his fan belt would have to be replaced. Rogan smiled and asked him to replace it. While this was being done he chatted with

Eric, and mentioned that he was in the computer manufacturing business and would be staying in Berlin for some time. He pretended not to see the sly, greedy interest on Eric Freisling's face. When Hans came in to tell him that the fan belt had been changed, Rogan tipped him generously and drove away. After he parked the Mercedes in front of his hotel he checked under the hood. The fan belt had not been changed.

Rogan made it a point to visit the gas station every few days in the Mercedes. The two Freislings, other than chiseling him on gas and oil, were showing an extraordinary friendliness. They had some other angle to work on him, Rogan knew, and wondered what it was. Certainly they had him pegged for a pigeon. But then he had plans for them too, he thought. Before he killed them, however, he would have to get from them the identity and whereabouts of the other three, especially the chief interrogator. Meanwhile he did not want to appear anxious and scare them off. He threw his money around as bait and waited for the Freislings to make their move.

The next weekend the hotel desk called early on Sunday evening to inform him that two men wished to come to his room. Rogan grinned at Rosalie. The brothers had taken the bait. But it was Rogan who was surprised. The two men were strangers. Or rather, one was a stranger. The taller of the two Rogan recognized almost immediately as Arthur Bailey, the American Intelligence agent who had interrogated Rogan about his "execution" and had asked him to identify suspects in Berlin more than nine years before. Bailey was studying Rogan with impassive eyes as he showed his identification.

"I just read up on your file, Mr. Rogan," Bailey said. "You don't look anything like your photographs anymore. I didn't recognize you at all when I first saw you again."

"When was that?" Rogan asked.

"At the Freisling gas station a week ago," Bailey said. He was a lanky midwestern type, his drawl as unmistakably American as were his clothes and posture. Rogan wondered why he hadn't noticed him at the gas station.

Bailey smiled gently at him. "We think the Freislings are East German agents, just as a sideline. They are hustlers. So when you showed up there and got friendly we checked you out. Called Washington, checked your visas and all that. Then I sat down and read your file. Something else clicked, and I went to the back files of the daily papers. And finally I figured it all out. You managed to track down those seven men in Munich, and now you've come back to knock them off. There was Moltke in Vienna and Pfann in Hamburg. The Freisling brothers are next on your list—right?"

"I'm here to sell computers," Rogan said warily. "That's all."

Bailey shrugged. "I don't care what you do; I'm not responsible for law enforcement in this country. But I'm telling you now: Hands off the Freisling brothers. I've put in a lot of time to get the goods on them, and when I do I'll bust up a whole East German spy setup. I don't want you knocking them off and leaving me with a blind trail."

Suddenly it was clear to Rogan why the Freisling brothers had been so friendly to him. "Are they after my data on the new computers?" he asked Bailey.

"I wouldn't be surprised," he said. "Computers—the new ones—are on the embargo list to Red countries. But I'm not worried about that; I know what you want to give them. And I'm warning you: You do, and you have me for an enemy."

Rogan stared at him coldly. "I don't know what you're talking about, but let me give you some advice: Don't get in my way or I'll run right over you. And there isn't a damn thing you can do to me. I've got pipelines right into the Pentagon. My new computers are more important to them than any crap you can drag up with a two-bit spy apparatus."

Bailey gave him a thoughtful look, then said, "OK, we can't touch you, but how about the girlfriend?" He jerked his head toward Rosalie sitting on the sofa. "We can sure as hell cause her a little trouble. In fact, one phone call and you'll never see her again."

"What the hell are you talking about?"

Bailey's lean, angular face took on an expression of mock surprise. "Didn't she tell you? Six months ago she escaped from a mental hospital on the Nordsee. She was committed in 1950 for schizophrenia. The authorities are still looking for her—not very hard, but looking. One phone call and the police pick her up. Just remember that." Bailey paused, and then said slowly, "When we don't need those two guys anymore I'll tell you. Why don't you skip them and go after the others that are still left?"

"Because I don't know who the other three are. I'm counting on the Freisling brothers to tell me."

Bailey shook his head. "They'll never talk unless you make it worth their while, and they're tough. You'd better leave it to us."

"No," Rogan said. "I have a surefire method. I'll make them talk. Then I'll leave them to you."

"Don't lie, Mr. Rogan. I know how you'll leave them." He put out his hand to shake Rogan's. "I've done my official duty, but after reading your file I have to wish you luck. Watch out for those Freisling brothers; they're a pair of sly bastards."

When Bailey and his silent partner had closed the door behind them Rogan turned to Rosalie. "Is it true what they said about you?"

Rosalie sat up straight, her hands folded in her lap. Her eyes gazed steadily into Rogan's. "Yes," she said.

They didn't go out that evening. Rogan ordered food and champagne to be sent up to their room, and after they finished they went to bed. Rosalie cradled her golden head in his arm and took puffs from his cigarette. "Shall I tell you about it?" she asked.

"If you want to," Rogan said. "It doesn't really make any difference, you know—your being sick."

"I'm all right now," she said.

Rogan kissed her gently. "I know."

"I want to tell you," she said. "Maybe you won't love me afterward, but I want to tell you."

"It doesn't matter," Rogan insisted. "It really doesn't."

Rosalie reached out and turned off the bedside table lamp. She could speak more freely in the dark.

CHAPTER 6

How she had wept that terrible day in the spring of 1945. The world had come to an end when she was a daydreaming fourteen-year-old maiden. The great dragon of war had carried her away.

She left her home early that morning to work on the family's rented garden plot on the outskirts of her hometown of Bublingshausen in Hesse. Later, she was digging the dark earth when a great shadow fell across the land. She looked up and saw a vast armada of planes blotting out the sun, and she heard the thunder of their bombs dropping on the optical works of Wetzlar. Then the bombs, overflowing as water overflows a glass, spilled into her own harmless medieval village. The badly frightened girl buried her face in the soft wormy earth as the ground trembled violently. When the sky no longer roared with thunder and the shadow had lifted from the sun, she made her way back to the heart of Bublingshausen.

It was burning. The gingerbread houses, like toys

torched by a wanton child, were melting down into ashes. Rosalie ran down the flowered streets she had known all her life, picking her way through smoldering rubble. It was a dream, she thought; how could all the houses she had known since childhood vanish so quickly?

And then she turned into the street that approached her home in the *Hintergasse*, and she saw a row of naked rooms, tier on tier. And it was magic that she could see the houses of her neighbors and friends without any shielding walls—the bedrooms, the dining rooms, all set before her like a play on the stage. And there was her mother's bedroom and her own kitchen that she had known all the fourteen years of her life.

Rosalie moved toward the entrance, but it was blocked by a hill of rubble. Sticking out of the vast pile of pulverized brick she saw the brown-booted feet and checked trouser legs that were her father's. She saw other bodies covered with red and white dust; and then she saw the one solitary arm pointing with mute agony toward the sky, on one gray finger the plaited gold band that was her mother's wedding ring.

Dazed, Rosalie sank down into the rubble. She felt no pain, no grief—only a peculiar numbness. The hours passed. Dusk was beginning to fall when she heard the continuous rumble of steel on crumbled stone. Looking up, she saw a long line of American tanks snaking through what had been Bublingshausen. They passed through the town and there was silence. Then a small Army truck with a canvas canopy came by. It stopped, and a young American soldier jumped down out of the driver's seat. He was blond and fresh-faced. He stood over her and said in rough German, "Hey, *Liebchen*, you want to come with us?"

Since there was nothing else to do, and since everyone she knew was dead, and since the garden she had planted that morning would not bear fruit for months, Rosalie went with the soldier in his canopied truck.

They drove until dark. Then the blond soldier took her into the back of the truck and made her lie down on a pile of army blankets. He knelt beside her. He broke open a bright green box and gave her a piece of hard round cheese and some chocolate. Then he stretched out beside her.

He was warm, and Rosalie knew that as long as she felt this warmth she could never die, never lie beneath the smoldering pile of rubbled brick where her mother and father now were. When the young soldier pressed against her and she felt the hard column of flesh against her thigh, she let him do whatever he wanted. Finally he left her huddled in the pile of blankets, and he went to the front and started to drive again.

During the night the truck stopped and other soldiers came into the back of it to lie on the blankets with her. She pretended to be asleep and let them, too, do as they wished. In the morning the truck continued on, then stopped in the heart of a great ruined city.

The air was sharper and colder. Rosalie recognized the dampness of the north, but though she had often read about Bremen in her schoolbooks she did not recognize this vast wasteland of bombed-out ruins as the famous merchant city.

The blond soldier helped her out of the truck and into a building whose lower floor was still intact. He took her into a huge dining room crammed with military gear and containing a black stove with a roaring fire. In the corner of the room was a bed with brown blankets. The blond soldier led her to the bed and told her to lie down on it. "My name is Roy," he said. And then he lowered himself upon her.

Rosalie spent the next three weeks in that bed. Roy curtained it with blankets so that it became a small private chamber. There Rosalie received an endless procession of faceless men who pushed themselves inside her. She didn't care. She was alive and warm. She was not cold beneath the rubble.

On the other side of the blanket curtain she could hear a great many male voices laughing; she could hear the shuffling of cards and the clink of bottles against glass. When one soldier left and another took his place, she always welcomed the new man with a smile and open arms. On one occasion a soldier peeped around the curtain and whistled with admiration when he saw her. She was already fully developed at fourteen, already a woman.

The soldiers treated her like a queen. They brought her heaped plates of food she had not tasted since before the war. The food seemed to stoke her body with unslakeable passion. She was a treasure of love, and they pampered her as they used her body. Once, the blond Roy who had picked her up in his truck said with concern, "Hey, baby, you wanta get some sleep? I'll chase everybody out." But she shook her head. For as long as her faceless lovers came through the curtain of blankets, she could believe it was all a dream—the hard flesh, her father's checked legs sticking out of the rubble, the wedding-banded hand pointing toward the sky. It could never come true.

But one day some other soldiers came, pistols on their hips, white helmets on their heads. They made her dress, then took her down to a truck loaded with other young girls, some joking, some crying. Rosalie must have fainted in the truck, for the next thing she knew she was lying in a hospital bed. Very dimly and from far away she saw a doctor looking at her intently. He had on a white jacket, but beneath it was an American uniform.

Lying on the cool white bed she heard the doctor say, "So this is the babe who has everything. Pregnant, too. We'll have to abort her. All that penicillin and fever killed the fetus. Such a beautiful kid, too."

Rosalie laughed. She knew she was dreaming beside her garden patch outside Bublingshausen, waiting to walk home to her father and mother. Perhaps there would be a letter from her older brother who was fighting in the East against Russia. But her dream was taking so long to end. She was frightened now, the dream was too terrible. She began to cry, and finally she was truly awake. . . .

Two doctors stood beside her hospital bed; one German, one American. The American smiled. "So you're back with us, young lady. That was close. Can you talk now?"

Rosalie nodded.

The American doctor said, "Do you know you put fifty American soldiers in the hospital with VD? You did more damage than a whole German regiment. Now—have you been with soldiers anywhere else?"

The German doctor leaned over to translate. Rosalie raised herself up on one arm, covers clutched modestly to her breast. She asked him gravely, "Then it's not a dream?" She saw his bewildered look. She started to weep. "I want to go home to my mother," she said. "I want to go home to Bublingshausen."

Four days later she was committed to the insane asylum at Nordsee.

In the darkness of their Berlin hotel room, Rogan pulled her close to him. He understood now about her emotional blankness, her apparent lack of any moral values. "Are you all right now?" he asked.

"Yes," she said. "Now I am."

CHAPTER 7

Rogan drove the Mercedes to the Freislings' gas station the next day and asked them to make some modifications on its body. Specifically he wanted the huge trunk in the rear to be made airtight. While the work was being done he became very chummy with the brothers, told them about his computer work and how his company was looking for an opportunity to sell their ideas to the countries behind the Iron Curtain. "Legally, of course, only legally," Rogan said in a tone of voice that implied he was just saying it for the record but that he would welcome a profitable crooked deal.

The two brothers smiled slyly. They understood. They questioned him more closely about his work. They asked him if he would be interested in making a tourist visit to East Berlin in their company. Rogan was delighted. "Of course," he said eagerly, and pressed them for a specific date. But they smiled and said, "*Langsam, langsam.* Slowly, slowly."

Several times they had seen Rosalie with him, and they had drooled over her beauty. Once when Rogan had gone into the office to pay a bill, he had come out to find Eric Freisling, with his head inside the Mercedes, talking earnestly to Rosalie. As they drove away Rogan asked Rosalie, "What did he say to you?"

Rosalie answered impassively, "He wanted me to sleep with him and spy on you."

Rogan didn't say anything. As he parked in front of the hotel Rosalie asked, "Which brother was it that talked to me? What is his name?"

"Eric," Rogan said.

Rosalie smiled at him sweetly. "When you kill them let me help you kill Eric."

The next day Rogan was busy making his own personal modifications on the Mercedes. He spent the rest of the week driving around Berlin and thinking out his plans. How would he make the Freisling brothers give him the names of the last three men? One day he went past the huge parking area of Berlin's main railway station. Thousands of cars were parked there. Rogan grinned. A perfect cemetery.

To build an image of being a big spender who had crude tastes—which in turn might suggest a moral corruptness—Rogan took Rosalie to the more expensive and disreputable nightclubs, night after night. He knew that the Freisling brothers, perhaps even the East German counterintelligence apparatus, would be checking him out.

When the Freislings arranged an East Berlin tourist visa for him and Rosalie, he expected the contact to be made then. He had in his pocket a sheaf of computer blueprints for sale. But no contact was made. They saw the concrete Headquarters Bunker in which Hitler had died. The Russians had tried to blow it up, but the concrete walls were so thick, so solid with cement and steel, that it had proved impossible to destroy. So this historic bomb shelter, which had witnessed the suicide of the most feared madman of all time, was now a grassy mound in the middle of a children's playground.

Strolling farther on through the Hansa quarter bristling with huge, gray, avant-garde apartment buildings, they were repelled by one of the new architectural gimmicks in the building complex. All its pipes for garbage, toilet waste, water, ended exposed in a huge glass terminal building, so that they looked like a nest of malignant steel snakes. Rosalie shuddered. "Let's go home," she said. She did not like the new world any better than the old.

Back in West Berlin they hurried to their hotel. Rogan unlocked the door to their suite and opened it for Rosalie, patting her round bottom as she went by. He followed her inside and heard her surprised gasp as he closed the door. He wheeled around.

They were waiting for him. The two Freisling brothers sat behind the coffee table, smoking cigarettes. It was Hans who spoke. "Herr Rogan, do not be alarmed. You understand that in our business one has to be careful. We did not wish anyone to know we had contacted you."

Rogan went forward to shake their hands. He smiled reassuringly. "I understand," he said. He understood more. That they had come early to search his room. To find out if he was a plant. To perhaps find and steal the blueprints so they would not have to pay cash for them—

Communist cash they could then put in their own pockets. But they had been out of luck and forced to wait. The blueprints were in his jacket pocket. More important, the seven envelopes, plus the gun and silencer, were in a small bag that he had checked into the hotel storage cellar.

Hans Freisling smiled. The last time he had smiled like that, his brother Eric had crept up behind Rogan to fire the bullet in his skull. "We wish to purchase some of your computer blueprints, in strict confidence of course. Are you agreeable?"

Rogan smiled back. "Have supper with me here tomorrow evening," he said. "You understand I have to make some arrangements. I do not keep everything I need in this room."

Eric Freisling smiled slyly and said, "We understand." He wanted Rogan to know that they had searched the suite; he wanted him to know that they were not men to be trifled with.

Rogan looked at him steadily. "Come tomorrow evening at eight," he said. He ushered them out of the room.

That night he could not respond to Rosalie, and when she finally fell asleep, Rogan lit a cigarette and waited for the familiar nightmare to come. He was on his third cigarette when it started.

And then in his mind a dark curtain was drawn aside and he was in the high-domed room of the Munich Palace of Justice. Far away in the limitless shadows of his brain seven men took their eternal shapes. Five of them were blurred; but two—Eric and Hans Freisling—were very clear, very distinct, as if they were standing in a spotlight. Eric's face was as he had looked into it that fatal day, the slack heavy mouth, the sly, snapping black eyes, the thick nose, and stamped over all the features, a brutish cruelty.

The face of Hans Freisling was similar to Eric's, but with cunning rather than cruelty in the expression. It was Hans who advanced on the young prisoner Rogan and encouraged him with false kindliness. It was Hans who looked directly into Rogan's eyes and reassured him. "Dress in those nice clothes," Hans had whispered. "We are going to set you free. The Americans are winning the war and some day you can help us. Remember how we spared your life. Change your clothes now. Quickly."

And then, trustfully, Rogan changed his clothing; gratefully he smiled at the seven murderers of his wife. When Hans Freisling put out his hand in friendship, the young prisoner Rogan reached out to grasp it. Only then did the faces of the five other men become clear with their furtive, guilty grins. And he thought: *Where is the seventh man?* And at that moment the brim of his new hat tilted forward over his eyes. He felt the cold metal of the gun barrel against the back of his neck. He felt his hair bristle with terror. And just before the bullet exploded in his skull he heard his cry for mercy, the long shrieking "Ahhhhhhhh." And the last thing he saw was Hans Freisling's sly smile of delight.

He must have cried out loud. Rosalie was awake. His whole body was shaking, absolutely out of control. Rosalie got up out of bed, and using a smooth cloth towel, she wiped his face with cooling alcohol. Then she bathed his whole body with it. Next, she ran the tub full of hot water and made him sit in the steaming bath. She sat on its marble rim as he soaked. Rogan could feel his body stop shaking, the pounding of blood against the metal plate in his skull easing off.

"Where did you learn all this?" he asked her.

Rosalie smiled. "The last three years in the asylum I was used as a nursing aide. I was almost well then. But it took me three years to get up enough courage to run away."

Rogan took her cigarette and puffed on it. "Why didn't they release you?"

She smiled down on him sadly. "They had no one to release me to," she said. "I have no one in the world." She paused for a long moment. "Except you."

The following day was a very busy one for Rogan. He gave Rosalie five hundred dollars' worth of marks and sent her out shopping. Then he went out to do some necessary chores. Making sure he was not followed, he drove to the outskirts of Berlin and parked the Mercedes. He went into a pharmacy and bought a small funnel and some chemicals. At a hardware store he bought wires, a small glass mixing bowl, nails, tape, and a few tools. He drove the Mercedes to a deserted side street, its ruins not yet rebuilt, and worked on the interior of the car for almost three hours. He disconnected all the wiring that operated the rear brake lights, and ran other wires into the car trunk. He bored holes into the airtight trunk, and then put tiny hollow rubber tubing into the holes. He mixed the chemicals, then put them in the small funnel and placed it over the piece of hollow tubing that now came up from the floor to the steering wheel. It was all very in-genious, and Rogan hoped it would work. He shrugged. If it didn't, he'd have to use the pistol and its silencer again. And that could be dangerous. It would hook him up with the other killings when the police compared bal-listic tests. Rogan shrugged again. The hell with it, he thought. By the time they got all the evidence together his mission would be completed.

He drove back to the hotel and parked in the special area reserved for guests. Before he went up to his room he drew his suitcase from the storage cellar. Rosalie was already waiting in their suite. It hadn't taken her long to spend the money. She modeled the seductive Paris gown she had bought, which scarcely covered her breasts. "If that doesn't distract those two bastards nothing will," Rogan said, with an exaggerated leer. "Now are you sure you know what you have to do tonight?"

Rosalie nodded, but he briefed her again, slowly and thoroughly. "Do you think they will tell you what you want to know?" Rosalie asked.

"I think so," Rogan said with a grim smile. "One way or the other." He picked up the telephone and ordered dinner for four to be sent up to the room at eight o'clock.

The Freisling brothers were punctual; they arrived with the food trolley. Rogan dismissed the waiter, and as they ate they discussed the terms of their deal. When they had finished eating he poured four glasses of *Pfefferminz* liqueur, half brandy, half peppermint. "Ah, my favorite drink," Hans Freisling said. Rogan smiled. He had re-membered the smell of peppermint in the interrogation room, the bottle Hans had carried around with him.

When Rogan capped the bottle he dropped in the drug pellets. He did it quickly and expertly; the brothers were not aware of what he was doing, though they were looking directly at him. With their natural suspiciousness, they were waiting for him to drink first. *"Prosit,"* Rogan said, and drank. The sweet liqueur almost made him sick. The two brothers drained their glasses, and Hans licked his thick lips greedily. Rogan passed him the bottle. "Help yourself," he said. "I must go and get the documents. Allow me." He went past them into the bedroom. As he did so he saw Hans fill his glass and drain it. Eric was not drinking. But then Rosalie leaned over, her creamy breasts showing. She filled Eric's glass for him and let her hand fall on his knee. Eric lifted the glass and drank, his eyes on Rosalie's breasts. Rogan closed the door of the bedroom behind him.

He opened the suitcase and took out the Walther pistol and its silencer. Quickly he fitted them together. Then holding the gun in plain view, he opened the door and walked back into the other room.

The drug in the liqueur was a slow-acting one, not a knockout drug. It was designed to cripple the victim's reflexes so that he would move and react very slowly. It was similar to the effect that too much alcohol has on a man's physical coordination, throwing it out of balance, yet leaving him the illusion that he is performing better than ever. So the Freisling brothers were not yet aware of what was happening to their bodies. When they saw the gun in Rogan's hands they both jumped up from their seats, but they moved in slow motion.

Rogan pushed them back onto their chairs. He sat

down opposite them. From his jacket pocket he took a flattened bullet, tarnished with age, and threw it on the coffee table between them.

"You, Eric," Rogan said. "You fired that bullet into the back of my skull ten years ago. In the Munich Palace of Justice. Do you remember me now? I'm the little playmate you sneaked up on while I was changing my clothes—and while your brother Hans kept telling me that I was going to be freed. I've changed a lot. Your bullet changed the shape of my head. But look hard. Do you recognize me now?" He paused, then said grimly, "I've come back to finish our little game together."

Mentally dulled by the drug, they both wore looks of blank incomprehension and stared at Rogan. It was Hans who first showed recognition, whose face first showed the natural shock, fear, and terrified surprise. Then they tried to flee, moving like men underwater. Rogan reached over and again gently pushed them back in their seats. He frisked them for weapons. They had none.

"Don't be afraid," Rogan said, deliberately imitating Hans' voice. "I'm not going to harm you." He paused. "Of course I'll turn you in to the authorities, but all I want from you now is a little information. As a long time ago you wanted some from me. I cooperated then, didn't I? I know you'll be just as intelligent."

Hans answered first, his voice thick with the drug but still sly. "Of course we'll cooperate; we'll tell you anything we know."

"But first we'll make a bargain," Eric growled sullenly.

As long as they kept sitting still the brothers seemed to function normally. Now Hans leaned forward and said with ingratiating friendliness, "Yes. What do you wish to know, and what will you do for us if we cooperate?"

Rogan said quietly, "I want to know the names of the other men who were with you in the Munich Palace of Justice. I want to know the name of the torturer who killed my wife."

Eric leaned over, parallel to his brother, and said slowly, contemptuously, "So you can kill us all like you killed Moltke and Pfann?"

"I killed them because they would not give me the other three names," Rogan said. "I offered them a chance to live as I now give you a chance to live." He signaled now to Rosalie. She brought over pads and pencils and handed them to the brothers.

Hans looked surprised, then grinned. "I will tell you right now. Their names are—" Before Hans could utter another word Rogan jumped up and smashed the German's mouth with the butt of his pistol. Hans' mouth became a dark hole out of which bloody pieces of gum bubbled, and bits of broken teeth. Eric tried to come to his brother's defense, but Rogan pushed him back into the chair. He did not trust himself to hit Eric. He was afraid he wouldn't stop until the man was dead.

"I don't want to hear any lies," Rogan said. "And to make sure you don't lie to me, you'll each—separately— write down the names of the other three men who were in the Munich Palace of Justice. You'll also put down where each man is living now. I'm especially interested in the chief interrogator. I also want to know which man actually killed my wife. When you've finished, I'll compare your separate lists. If both have the same names, you won't be killed. If the information does not tally, if you have different names listed, you'll both be killed immediately. That's the deal. It's up to you."

Hans Freisling was gagging, clawing pieces of broken teeth and bits of gum from his smashed mouth. He couldn't speak. Eric asked the final question: "If we cooperate, what will you do to us?"

Rogan tried to sound as earnest and sincere as possible. "If you both write down the same information, I won't kill you. I'll accuse you as war criminals, however, and turn you in to the proper authorities. Then you'll have to stand trial and take your chances."

He was amused by the secret looks they gave each other and knew just what they were thinking. Even if arrested and tried, even if convicted, they could appeal and get out on bail. Then they figured they could defect to East Germany and thumb their noses at justice. Rogan, pretending not to notice the looks they exchanged, pulled Hans out of his chair and moved him to the other end of the coffee table so that neither one could see what his brother was writing down. "Get busy," he said. "And it had better be good. Or you'll both die here in this room, tonight." He pointed the Walther pistol at Eric's head while keeping Hans in full view. With the silencer, the pistol was a frightening-looking weapon.

The brothers began to write. Hampered by the drug, they wrote laboriously, and it seemed a long time before first Eric, then Hans, finished. Rosalie, who had sat on the coffee table between them to make certain they could not signal to each other, picked up their pads to hand them to Rogan. He shook his head. "Read them to me," he said. He kept the pistol pointed at Eric's head. He had already decided to kill him first.

Rosalie read Eric's list aloud. "Our commanding officer was Klaus von Osteen. He is now chief justice in the Munich courts. The other two were observers. The man from the Hungarian army was Wenta Pajerski. He is now a Red party chief in Budapest. The third man was Genco Bari. He was an observer from the Italian army. He now lives in Sicily."

Rosalie paused. She switched the pads to read what Hans had written. Rogan held his breath. "Klaus von Osteen was the commanding officer. He was the one who killed your wife." Rosalie paused at the look of anguish that passed over Rogan's face. Then she continued reading.

The information tallied—both brothers had put down essentially the same information, the same names, although only Hans had named Christine's murderer. And as Rogan compared the two pads he realized that Eric had given the minimum of information, whereas Hans had included extra details such as Genco Bari being a Mafia member, probably a big man in the organization. Rogan, however, had the feeling that the brothers had held back something he should know about. They were exchanging sly, congratulatory looks.

Again Rogan pretended not to notice. "OK," he said. "You did the smart thing, so I'm going to keep my part of the bargain. Now I must turn you over to the police. We'll leave this room together and go down the back stairs. Remember, don't try to run. I'll be right behind you. If you recognize anyone when we get outside, don't try to signal them."

The two men looked unconcerned; Eric was smirking at Rogan quite openly. Rogan was a fool, they thought. Didn't the Amerikaner realize the police would release them immediately?

Rogan played it very straight and very dumb. "One other thing," he said. "Downstairs I'm going to put you in the trunk of my car." He saw the fear in their faces. "Don't be frightened and don't make a fuss. How can I control you if I have to drive the car?" he asked reasonably. "How else can I conceal you from any friends who may be waiting for you outside when I drive out of the parking lot?"

Eric snarled, "We made the trunk of that car an airsealed chamber. We'll suffocate. You plan to kill us anyway."

"I've had special air holes drilled into the trunk since then," Rogan said blandly.

Eric spat on the floor. He made a sudden grab for Rosalie and held her in front of him. But the drug had so weakened him that Rosalie easily twisted out of his grasp. And as she wrenched free one of her long painted fingernails went into Eric's eye. He screamed and held his hand to his left eye. Rosalie stepped out of the line of fire.

Up to this moment Rogan had controlled his anger. Now his head began to throb with familiar pain. "You dirty bastard," he said to Eric. "You put down as little information as possible. You didn't tell me it was Klaus von Osteen who killed my wife. And I'm willing to bet you helped him. Now you don't want to get into the trunk of the car because you think I'm going to kill you. All right, you son of a bitch. I'm going to kill you right now. Right here in the hotel room. I'm going to beat you to a bloody pulp. Or maybe I'll just blow your head off."

It was Hans who brought peace. Almost tearfully, through his puffed and bloody lips, he said to his brother, "Be calm, do what the American wishes us to do. Don't you see he has gone mad?"

Eric Freisling looked searchingly at Rogan's face. "Yes," he said then. "I will do what you wish."

Rogan stood very still. Rosalie came up beside him and touched him as if to bring him back to sanity. And his terrible anger began to subside. He said to her, "You know what you have to do after we leave?"

"Yes."

Rogan herded the two brothers out of the room and down the back stairs of the hotel. He kept the gun in his pocket. When they went out of the rear entrance that led to the parking lot, Rogan whispered directions until they came to where the Mercedes was parked. Rogan made them kneel in the gravel at his feet while he unlocked the trunk. Eric got into it first, awkwardly, the drug still affecting his movements. He gave Rogan a last distrustful look. Rogan pushed him to the floor. As Hans crawled into the spacious trunk his mouth tried to form a smile; it was an obscene leer because of his smashed lips and fragmented teeth. He said meekly, humbly, "You know, I'm glad this happened. All these years what we did to you has been on my conscience. I think it will be very good for me, psychologically, to be punished."

"Do you really think so?" Rogan said politely, and slammed the trunk lid down over them.

CHAPTER 8

Rogan drove the Mercedes around Berlin for the next couple of hours. He made sure a supply of air was going through the rubber hosing and into the trunk. This was to give Rosalie time to do her part. She had to go down to the hotel ballroom, where she would drink, flirt, and dance with the unattached men so that later everyone would remember her having been there. This would give her an alibi.

Near midnight Rogan pulled the wire attached to the steering wheel. This would cut off the air and feed carbon monoxide into the trunk. In thirty minutes or less the Freisling brothers would be dead. Rogan now drove toward the Berlin railway station.

But after fifteen minutes Rogan stopped the car. He had intended to kill them as they had tried to kill him in the Munich Palace of Justice, without warning and still hoping for freedom. He had meant to slaughter them like animals, but he could not.

He got out of the car, went around to the back, and banged on the trunk lid. "Hans . . . Eric," he called. He didn't know why he used their first names, as if they had become friends. He called out again, in a low urgent voice, to warn them they were going into the eternal darkness of death, so that they could compose whatever souls they had, say whatever prayers possible to make themselves ready for the black void. Again he banged on the trunk, louder this time, but there was no answer. He realized suddenly what must have happened. In their drugged condition they had probably died shortly after Rogan had switched to the carbon monoxide. To make sure that they were dead and not shamming, Rogan unlocked the trunk and raised the lid.

Evil they had been, no loss to the world, but in their last moments they had found some spark of humanity. In their final agony the two brothers had turned to each other and died in each other's arms. Their faces had lost all slyness and cunning. Rogan stared at them for a long time. It was a mistake, he thought, to have killed them together. Accidentally, he had been merciful.

He locked the trunk and drove on to the railway station. He swung the car into the vast car park, filled with thousands of vehicles, and parked it in the section he thought most likely to remain filled, near the east entrance. Then he got out of the Mercedes and started toward his hotel. As he walked he let the keys to the Mercedes slip out of his hand and into the gutter.

He walked all the way back to the hotel, and so it was nearly three in the morning before he let himself into his hotel suite. Rosalie was waiting up for him. She brought him a glass of water to take with his pills, but Rogan could feel the blood pounding in his head, louder and louder. The familiar sickish, sweet taste was in his mouth, and then he felt the fearsome spinning vertigo, and he was falling . . . falling . . . falling. . . .

CHAPTER 9

It was three days before Rogan became conscious of his surroundings. He was still in the hotel suite, lying in his bed, but the bedroom had the antiseptic smell of a hospital. Rosalie was hovering over him, instantly at his side when she saw he was awake. Peering over her shoulder was a peevish-faced man with a beard who resembled the comical German doctor in films.

"Ah"—the doctor's voice was a harsh voice—"you have finally found your way back to us. Fortunate, very fortunate. Now I must insist you go to the hospital."

Rogan shook his head. "I'm OK here. Just give me a prescription for some more of my pills. No hospital is going to help me."

The doctor adjusted his spectacles and stroked his beard. Despite the facial camouflage he looked young, and he was obviously disturbed by Rosalie's beauty. Now he turned to scold her. "You must give this fellow some peace. He is suffering from nervous exhaustion. He must have complete rest for at least two weeks. Do you understand me?" The young doctor angrily tore a sheet from his prescription pad and handed it to her.

There was a knock on the door of the hotel suite, and Rosalie went to answer it. The American Intelligence agent Bailey came in, followed by two German detectives. Bailey's long Gary Cooper face was sour. "Where's your boyfriend?" he asked Rosalie. She nodded toward the bedroom door. The three men moved toward it.

"He's sick," Rosalie said. But the three men went into the bedroom.

Bailey did not seem surprised to find Rogan in bed. Neither did he seem to have any sympathy for the sick man. He looked down at Rogan and said flatly, "So you went ahead and did it."

"Did what?" Rogan asked. He was feeling fine now. He grinned up at Bailey.

"Don't bullshit me," Bailey snapped angrily. "The Freisling brothers have disappeared. Just like that. They left their gas station closed; their stuff is still in their apartment; their money is still in the bank. That means only one thing: They're dead."

"Not necessarily," Rogan said.

Bailey waved his hand impatiently. "You'll have to answer some questions. These two men are from the German political police. You'll have to get dressed and come down to their headquarters."

The young bearded doctor spoke up. His voice was angry, commanding. "This man cannot be moved."

One of the German detectives said to him, "Watch

yourself. You don't want all those years in medical school to be wasted on a pick and shovel."

Instead of frightening the doctor, this made him angrier. "If you move this man he may very well die. I will then personally press charges of manslaughter against you and your department."

The German detectives, astonished at this defiance, did not say another word. Bailey studied the doctor and said, "What's your name?"

The doctor bowed, almost clicked his heels, and said, "Thulman. At your service. And what is your name, sir?"

Bailey gave him a long intimidating stare; then, in obvious mockery, he bowed and clicked his heels together. "Bailey," he said. "And we are going to take this man down to the *Halle*."

The doctor gave him a look of contempt. "I can click my heels together louder than you when I am barefooted, you poor imitation of a Prussian aristocrat. But that is beside the point. I forbid you to move this man because he is ill; his health will be severely endangered. I do not think you can afford to disregard my warnings."

Rogan could see that the three men were baffled. He was, too. Why the hell was this doctor sticking his neck out for him?

Bailey said sarcastically, "Will it kill him if I ask him a few questions right here and now?"

"No," said the doctor, "but it will tire him."

Bailey made an impatient gesture and turned his lanky frame toward Rogan. "Your visas for travel in Germany are being revoked," he said. "I've had that arranged. I don't care what you do in any other country, but I want you out of my territory. Don't try to come back with phony papers. I'll have my eye on you as long as you're in Europe. Right now you can thank this doctor for saving your ass." Bailey walked out of the bedroom, the two German detectives followed, and Rosalie ushered all three out of the suite.

Rogan grinned at the doctor. "Is it true—I really can't be moved?"

The young doctor stroked his beard. "Of course. However, you may move yourself, since then there would be no psychological stress on your nervous system." He smiled at Rogan. "I dislike seeing healthy men, especially policemen, bully sick people. I don't know what you are up to, but I'm on your side."

Rosalie saw the doctor to the door, then came back and sat on the bed. Rogan put his hand over hers. "Do you still want to stay with me?" he asked. She nodded. "Then pack all our things," Rogan said. "We'll leave for Munich. I want to meet Klaus von Osteen before the others. He's the most important one."

Rosalie bowed her head to his. "They will kill you after all," she said.

Rogan kissed her. "That's why I have to take care of von Osteen first. I want to make sure of him. I don't mind so much if the other two get away." He gave her a gentle push. "Start packing," he said.

They caught a morning flight to Munich and checked into a small pension where Rogan hoped they might not be noticed. He knew that Bailey and the German police would trace him to Munich, but it would take them a few days to discover his whereabouts. By then his mission would be completed and he would be out of the country.

He rented a small Opel while Rosalie went to the library to read up on von Osteen in the newspaper file and to locate his home address.

When they met for dinner, Rosalie had a full report. Klaus von Osteen was now the highest-ranking judge of the Munich courts. He had started off as the wastrel son of a famous noble family related to the English royal family. Though he had been a German officer during the war, there was no record of his having joined the Nazi party. Shortly before the end of the war he had been severely wounded and that had apparently turned him into a new man at the age of forty-three. Back in civilian life he had studied law and had become one of the best lawyers in Germany. He had then entered the political arena as a moderate and a supporter of the American entente in Europe. Great things were expected of him; it was possible that he might even become the chancellor of West Germany. He had the support of the German industrialists and the American occupation authorities, and a magnetic influence over the working classes as a superb orator.

Rogan nodded grimly. "That sounds like the guy. He had a terrific voice, sincere as hell. The bastard really covered his tracks, though."

Rosalie said anxiously, "Are you sure this is the right man?"

"It's the right one; it has to be," Rogan said. "How could Eric and Hans hit on the same name unless it was the truth?" He paused. "We'll go to his house right after dinner. When I see his face I'll recognize him, no matter how much he's changed. But it's him, all right. He was a real aristocrat."

They drove to von Osteen's address, using a city map as a guide. Von Osteen's house was in a fashionable suburb, and it was a mansion. Rogan parked the car and they went up the stone steps to the huge baronial doors. There was a wooden knocker in the shape of a wild boar's head. Rogan slammed it twice against the wooden panel. In a moment the door was opened by an old-fashioned German butler, grossly fat, obsequious. Very coldly he said, *"Bitte mein Herr."*

"We have come to see Klaus von Osteen," Rogan said. "On confidential business. Just tell him that Eric Freisling sent us."

The butler's voice was less cold. He evidently recognized the Freisling name. "It is regrettable," he said. "Judge von Osteen and the family are on vacation in Switzerland, and then they plan to go to Sweden and Norway and finally England. They will not be back for nearly a month."

"Damn," Rogan said. "Can you tell me where they are staying right now—their address?"

The butler smiled, his face creasing into ridges of ruddy suet. "No," he said. "Judge von Osteen is not following a schedule. He can be reached only through official channels. Do you wish to leave a message, sir?"

"No," Rogan said. He and Rosalie returned to the car.

Back in their room, Rosalie asked, "What will you do now?"

"I'll have to gamble," he said. "I'll go to Sicily and

track down Genco Bari. If everything works out OK, I'll fly to Budapest and see about Wenta Pajerski. Then I'll come back to von Osteen here in Munich."

Rosalie said, "What about your entry visa? Bailey will have that canceled."

Rogan said drily, "I used to be in the spy business too. I'll find a way to get a phony passport or a phony visa. And if Bailey gets too close, I'll just have to forget he's a fellow American."

Rosalie said, "What about me?"

He didn't answer her for a long time. "I'm making arrangements so that you'll get enough money to live on every month. A trust fund that will go on, no matter what happens."

"You're not taking me with you?" Rosalie asked.

"I can't," Rogan said. "I'd have to get you papers. And I'd never be able to lose Bailey if I took you along."

"Then I'll wait for you here in Munich," she said.

"OK. But you have to get used to the idea of my not being around some time. The chances are a million to one against my making it all the way. They'll nail me for sure when I get von Osteen."

Gratefully she leaned her head against his shoulder. "I don't care," she said. "Just let me wait for you; please let me wait for you."

He stroked her blond hair. "Sure, sure," he said. "Now will you do something for me?"

She nodded.

"I was looking at the map," Rogan said. "We can drive to Bublingshausen in four hours. I think it would be good for you to see it again. Will you go back?"

He felt her whole body go tense, her back arch in terror. "Oh, no," she said. "Oh, no!"

He held her quivering body close. "We'll drive through very quickly," he said. "You'll see how it is. Now. Then maybe you won't see so clearly how it was before. Maybe everything will blur. Try. I'll drive through very fast, I promise. Remember, that's the first thing you told the doctor—that you wanted to go back to Bublingshausen?"

Her body had stopped shaking. "All right," she said. "I'll go back. With you."

CHAPTER 10

The next morning they loaded the Opel with Rogan's things. They had decided that from Bublingshausen they would drive on to Frankfurt, where Rogan could catch a plane to Sicily and look for Genco Bari. Rosalie would take the train back to Munich and wait for Rogan there. Rogan had reassured her. "When I finish in Sicily and Budapest I'll come back here for Osteen. And I'll come straight to the pension, first thing." In this he had lied. He planned to see her again only if he killed von Osteen and managed to stay free.

The Opel sped along the German roads. Rosalie sat as far away from Rogan as possible, huddled against her door, head turned away. Near midday Rogan asked, "Do you want to stop for lunch?" She shook her head. As they came nearer and nearer to Bublingshausen, Rosalie hunched farther and farther down in her seat. Rogan swung the Opel off the main *autobahn*, and then they were entering the city of Wetzlar, whose great optical works had been the original target of the American bombers that had killed her father and mother. The Opel moved slowly through the heavy city traffic, then finally came to the yellow sign, with its arrow pointed toward the suburban road, that read "Bublingshausen." Rosalie buried her face in her hands so that she would not be able to see.

Rogan drove slowly. When they entered the village he studied it carefully. There were no scars of war. It had been completely rebuilt, only the houses were no longer made of gingerbread wood, but of concrete and steel. Children played in the streets. "We're here," he said. "Look up."

Rosalie kept her head in her hands. She didn't answer. Rogan made the car go very slowly, easier to control; then he reached over and pulled Rosalie's blond head out of her hands, forcing her to look at her childhood village.

What happened then surprised him. She turned on him with anger and said, "This is not my village. You've made a mistake. I don't recognize anything here." But then the street made a turn, heading out toward open country, and there were the fenced-in plots of ground, private gardens, each gate with its owner's name printed on a varnished yellow board. Wildly Rosalie turned her head to look back at the village, then at the gardens. He could see the recognition dawning in her eyes. She started fumbling with the door handle and Rogan stopped the car. Then Rosalie was out and running across the road onto the grassy earth of the gardens, running awkwardly. She stopped and looked up into the sky, and then finally she turned her head toward Bublingshausen. Rogan could see her body arch with her inward agony, and when she crumpled to the ground he got out of the car and ran to her.

She was sitting awkwardly, legs splayed out, and she was weeping. Rogan had never seen anyone weep with such grief. She was wailing like a small child, wailing that would have been comical if it had not been so powerfully wrung from her guts. She tore at the earth with her painted fingernails, as if she were trying to inflict pain on it. Rogan stood beside her, waiting, but she gave no sign that she knew he was there.

Two young girls, no more than fourteen, came down the road from Bublingshausen. They carried gardening sacks over their arms and they chatted gaily together. They entered the gates of their families' gardens and began digging. Rosalie raised her head to watch them, and they gave her curious, envious glances. Envious of her fine clothes, envious of the obviously wealthy man who stood beside her. Rosalie stopped weeping. She tucked her legs beneath her and put a hand on Rogan's leg to make him sit on the grass beside her.

Then she cradled her head against his shoulder and wept quietly for a very long time. He understood that finally now, for the first time, she could grieve for her lost father and mother, her brother in his cold Russian grave. And he understood that as a young girl she had gone into some terrible shock that prevented her from consciously accepting her loss, but that had instead driven her into schizophrenia and the asylum. She had a chance now to get over it, Rogan thought.

When she had finished weeping, Rosalie sat for a

while staring at the village of Bublingshausen and then at the two young girls digging in their gardens. The girls kept glancing up at Rosalie, devouring her expensive clothes with their eyes, coolly inspecting her beauty.

Rogan helped Rosalie to her feet. "Those two girls envy you," he said.

She nodded and smiled sadly. "I envy them."

They drove on to Frankfurt and Rogan returned the car to the rental agency office at the airport. Rosalie waited with him until takeoff time. Before he walked down the ramp, she said to him, "Can't you forget the rest of them; can't you let them live?"

Rogan shook his head.

Rosalie clung to him. "If I lose you now it would be the end of me. I know it. Please let the others go."

Rogan said gently, "I can't. Maybe I could forget about Genco Bari and the Hungarian, Wenta Pajerski. But I could never forgive Klaus von Osteen. And since I have to kill him, I have to kill the others. That's the way it is."

She still clung to him. "Let von Osteen go," she said. "It doesn't matter. Let him stay alive and then you'll stay alive, and I'll be happy, I can live happily."

"I can't," he said.

"I know. He killed your wife and he tried to kill you. But everybody was trying to kill each other then." She shook her head. "Their crime against you was murder. But it was everybody's crime then. You would have to kill the whole world to get your revenge."

Rogan pushed her away from him. "I know all that, everything you've just said. I've thought about it all these years. I might have forgiven them for killing and torturing Christine. I might have forgiven them for torturing and trying to kill me. But von Osteen did something that I can never forgive. He did something to me that makes it impossible for me to live on the same planet with him, as long as he's alive. He destroyed me without bullets, without even raising his voice. He was crueler than all the others." Rogan paused, and he could feel the blood begin to pound against the plate in his skull. "In my dreams I kill him, and then I bring him back to life so I can kill him again."

They were calling the number of his flight over the loudspeaker. Rosalie kissed him hurriedly and whispered, "I'll wait in Munich for you. In the same pension. Don't forget me."

Rogan kissed her eyes and mouth. "For the first time I hope I come through it alive," he said. "Before, I didn't care. I won't forget you." He turned and walked down the ramp to the plane.

CHAPTER 11

Flying over Germany in twilight, Rogan could see how the country had rebuilt itself. The rubbled cities of 1945 had sprung back with more factory smokestacks, taller steel spires. But there were still ugly scabs of burned-out sections visible from the sky, the pockmarks of war.

He was in Palermo and checked into its finest hotel before midnight, already starting his search. He had asked the hotel manager if he knew anyone in the city by the name of Genco Bari. The hotel manager had shrugged and spread his arms wide. Palermo, after all, had over 400,000 people. He could hardly be expected to know all of them, could he, *signore*?

The next morning, Rogan contracted a firm of private detectives to track down Genco Bari. He gave them a generous retainer and promised them a large bonus if they were successful. Then he made the rounds of those official bureaux he thought might help him. He went to the United States consulate, the Sicilian chief of police, the publishing office of Palermo's biggest newspaper. None of them knew anything of or anyone named Genco Bari.

It seemed impossible to Rogan that his search would not be successful. Genco Bari must be a wealthy man, a man of substance, since he was a member of the Mafia. Then he realized that this was the hitch. Nobody, no one at all would give him information on a Mafia chief. In Sicily the law of *omertà* ruled. *Omertà*, the code of silence, was an ancient tradition of these people: Never give information of any kind to any of the authorities. The punishment for breaking the code was swift and sure death, and not to be risked to satisfy the mere curiosity of a foreigner. In the face of *omertà* the police chief and the firm of private detectives were helpless in their quest for information. Or perhaps they, too, did not break the unwritten law.

At the end of the first week, Rogan was about to move on to Budapest when he received a surprise caller at his hotel. It was Arthur Bailey, the Berlin-based American Intelligence agent.

Bailey held out a protesting hand, a friendly smile on his face. "I'm here to help," he said. "I found out you've got too much drag in Washington to be pushed around, so I might as well. Of course I have my selfish motive, too. I want to keep you from accidentally ruining a lot of our groundwork in setting up information systems in Europe."

Rogan looked at him thoughtfully for a long moment. It was impossible to doubt the man's sincerity and warm friendliness. "Fine," he said at last. "You can start off helping me by telling me where to find Genco Bari." He offered the lean American a drink.

Bailey sat down, relaxed, and sipped his Scotch. "Sure, I can tell you that," he said. "But first you have to promise that you'll let me help you all the way. After Genco Bari you'll go after Pajerski in Budapest and then von Osteen in Munich, or vice versa. I want you to promise to follow my advice. I don't want you caught. If you are, you'll wreck Intelligence contacts it's taken the United States years and millions of dollars to set up."

Rogan didn't smile or act particularly friendly. "OK. Just tell me where Bari is—and make sure I get a visa for Budapest."

Bailey sipped his drink. "Genco Bari is living in his walled estate just outside the village of Villalba in central Sicily. The necessary Hungarian visas will be waiting for you in Rome whenever you're ready. And in Budapest I want you to contact the Hungarian interpreter at the United States consulate. His name is Rakol. He'll give you all the help you need and arrange your exit from the country. Fair enough?"

"Sure," Rogan said. "And when I get back to Munich do I contact you, or will you contact me?"

"I'll contact you," Bailey said. "Don't worry. I'll be able to find you."

Bailey finished his drink. Rogan saw him to the elevator and Bailey said casually, "After you killed those first four guys, that gave us enough of a lead to break your Munich Palace of Justice case wide open. That's how I know about Bari, Pajerski, and von Osteen."

Rogan smiled politely. "That's what I figured," he said. "But since I found them by myself, it doesn't matter what you found out. Right?"

Bailey gave him an odd look, shook hands, and just before getting into the elevator said, "Good luck."

As Bailey knew the whereabouts of Genco Bari, Rogan realized that everyone else must have known too—the police chief, the private detectives, probably even the hotel manager. Genco Bari was one of the big Mafia leaders of Sicily; his name was no doubt known throughout the country.

He rented a car to drive the fifty-odd miles to Villalba. It struck him that he would quite possibly never leave this island alive, and that the last criminals would remain unpunished. But that didn't seem to matter so much now. As it did not matter that he had made up his mind not to see Rosalie again. He had arranged for her to receive money from his estate once she had been in touch with the office. She would forget about him and make a new life. Nothing mattered at the moment except killing Genco Bari. And Rogan thought about that man in the Italian uniform. The only man of the seven in the high-domed room in the Munich Palace of Justice who had treated him with any genuine warmth. And yet he, too, had taken part in the final betrayal.

On that final terrible morning in the Munich Palace of Justice, Klaus von Osteen had smiled in the shadows behind his great desk, as Hans and Eric Freisling had urged Rogan to change into his "freedom clothes." Genco Bari had said nothing; he'd merely looked at him with gentle pitying eyes. Finally he had crossed the room and stood in front of Rogan. He had helped Rogan knot his tie, had patted it securely inside Rogan's jacket. He had distracted Rogan so that Rogan had never seen Eric Freisling slip behind him with the gun. Bari, too, had taken a hand in the final humiliating cruelty of the execution. And it was because of Bari's humanity that Rogan could not forgive him. Moltke had been a selfish, self-serving man; Karl Pfann, a brutal animal. The Freisling brothers were evil incarnate. What they had done could be expected, springing as it did out of their very natures. But Genco Bari had exuded a human warmth, and his taking part in torture and execution was a deliberate, malignant degeneracy; unforgivable.

Now driving through the starry Sicilian night, Rogan thought of all the years he had dreamed of his revenge. How it had been the one thing that had kept him from dying. And when they had thrown him on the pile of corpses stacked outside the Munich Palace of Justice, even then when his shattered brain oozed blood and flickered with only a tiny spark, how that tiny spark had been kept alive by the energy of sheer hatred.

And now that he was no longer with Rosalie, now that he planned not to see her again, his memories of his dead wife seemed to flood back into his being. He thought, Christine, Christine, you would have loved this starry night, the balmy air of Sicily. You always trusted and liked everyone. You never understood the work I was doing, not really. You never understood what would happen to all of us if we were captured. When I heard your screams in the Munich Palace of Justice, it was the surprise in your screams that made them so terrifying. You could not believe that human beings did such terrible things to their fellow human beings.

She had been beautiful: long legs for a French girl, with rounded thighs; a slim waist and small shy breasts that grew bold beneath his hand; lovely soft brown hair like overflowing silk; and charmingly serious eyes. Her lips, full and sensual, had had the same character and honesty as he'd seen in her eyes.

What had they done to her before she died? Bari, Pfann, Moltke, the Freislings, Pajerski, and von Osteen? How had they made her scream so; how had they killed her? He had never asked any of the others because they would have lied to him. Pfann and Moltke would have made it seem less terrible; the Freisling brothers would have invented gory details to make him suffer even now. Only Genco Bari would tell him the truth. For some reason Rogan was sure of this. He would finally learn how his pregnant wife had died. He would learn what had caused those terrible screams, the screams that the torturers had recorded and preserved so carefully.

CHAPTER 12

He reached the town of Villalba at 11:30 p.m. and was surprised to find it brilliantly lighted, hundreds of colored lanterns strung in arches over every street. From gaily decorated wooden booths lining the cobblestone pavements, villagers offered hot sausages for sale, and wine, and thick Sicilian pizza squares with oily anchovies buried in a rich bed of tomato sauce. The smell filled the night air and made Rogan ravenous. He stopped the car and devoured a sandwich of sausage until his mouth felt on fire from the hot spicy meat. Then he moved to the next booth to buy a glass of tart red wine.

He had come to Villalba on the birthday of the town's patron saint, Saint Cecilia. As was the custom, the people of the town were celebrating the birthday of their saint with a great fiesta that would last three days. Rogan had arrived on the evening of the fiesta's second day. By this time everybody, including some of the small children, was drunk on the new, tart Sicilian wine. They greeted Rogan with open arms. And when they heard him speak his almost perfect Italian the wine merchant, a huge fat man with big mustaches who said his name was Tullio, embraced Rogan.

They drank together. Tullio wouldn't let him go, refused to take money for the wine. Other men gathered around. Some brought long loaves of bread stuffed with sweet fried peppers; others gnawed on smoked eels. Children danced in the streets. Then down the main avenue came three elaborately dressed girls, shining black hair piled high, strolling arm in arm and giving the men provocative looks. These were the fiesta *putains,* the festival whores, specially picked and imported to pluck the virginity of all the young men who had come of age this year, and thus protect the honor of the local girls.

The men around the wine booth melted away, joining the long trail of young men following the three fiesta *putains.*

The fiesta would be a great cover, Rogan thought. He might be able to do the job this very night and be out of town by morning. He asked Tullio, "Can you tell me where the house of Genco Bari is located?"

The change in the huge Sicilian was immediate. His face froze into a blank mask. All friendliness vanished. "I do not know any Genco Bari," he said.

Rogan laughed. "I am an old war comrade of his, and he invited me to visit him here in Villalba. Never mind, I'll find it myself."

Tullio immediately unfroze. "Ah, you are invited to his fiesta also? The whole village is invited. Come, I'll go with you myself." And though there were at least five customers waiting for wine, Tullio motioned them away and shuttered the wooden booth. Then he took Rogan by the arm and said, "Put yourself in my hands and you will never forget this night as long as you live."

"I hope so," Rogan said politely.

The villa of Genco Bari, on the outskirts of the town, was surrounded by a high stone wall. The two huge iron grille gates had been swung open, and the grounds of the just visible mansion were decorated with colored streamers that went from tree to tree. Genco Bari was holding open house for the villagers, most of whom worked on his farmlands. Rogan followed Tullio inside the gates.

Long garden tables were laden with great bowls of macaroni, fruit, and homemade ice cream. Women filled glasses from wine casks resting on the lawn, and offered the red-purple liquid to anyone who passed by. The whole surrounding countryside seemed to be attending the fête here on the grounds of the Mafia leader's estate. On a raised platform three musicians began a wild piping dance tune. And on the same raised platform, seated on a thronelike carved chair, was the man Rogan had come to kill.

The Mafia leader shook hands with everyone. He smiled graciously. But Rogan almost did not recognize him. The fleshy tanned face had changed to a bony waxen death's-head the color of the faded ice cream Panama hat that adorned the shrunken head. Amidst the gaiety of the fiesta, Genco Bari was the white mask of death. There was no doubt: Rogan would have to move fast to claim his revenge, or a more impersonal executioner would do the job.

Men and women formed into a square to dance to the music. Rogan became separated from Tullio as he was swept into the vortex of the dance. He seemed to descend into a whirling funnel of human bodies that spewed him out into the open air, hand in hand with a young Sicilian girl. Other couples were peeling off from the whirling crowd and disappearing into the bushes. Rogan's girl danced behind a huge wine barrel and drank from a great silver pitcher on top of it. Then she held up the pitcher for Rogan to drink.

She was beautiful. Her full sensuous mouth was stained purple from wine. Her flashing dark eyes, her clear olive skin, consumed the lantern light in their own greater fire. Her full breasts, spilling over the low-cut blouse, pulsated with her eager breathing, and her plump thighs strained against the silk skirt, the hungry flesh not to be denied or contained. She watched Rogan drink, pushing her body up to his; then she led him through dark treelined lanes, away from the festivities, to the rear of the stone mansion. He followed her up a flight of outside stone steps that spiraled along the walls and ended at a balcony. Then they were going through inky glass doors to an inside bedroom.

The girl turned and held up her mouth to Rogan. Her breasts were heaving with passion, and Rogan put his hands on them as if to still their movement. Her arms twined around his body, pressing him close.

For a moment Rogan thought of Rosalie. He had made up his mind that he would not see her again, that he would not let her share what he was sure would be his capture or death. Now, by making love to this girl, the decision would become final in his mind. And more important, the girl was the key to penetrating Genco Bari's mansion; he was in it right now. With the girl, who was growing impatient.

She was pulling him onto the bed, tugging at his clothes. Her skirt was hiked up to her stomach, and Rogan could see her marvelous full-fleshed thighs, feel her hot skin burning his own. In minutes they were coiled about each other like two snakes, twisting on the bed, straining and plunging, their naked bodies slippery with sweat, until finally they rolled onto the cool stone floor. Locked in each other's arms they fell asleep there, woke, drank red wine from a jug, got back on the bed, made love again, and fell asleep for a final time.

When Rogan woke up in the morning he had the worst hangover of his life. He felt as if his whole body was filled with sweet rotten grapes. He groaned, and the naked girl next to him cooed sympathetically, reached down beneath the bed, and lifted up the half-empty jug of wine they had been drinking the night before.

"This is the only cure," she said. She drank from the jug and handed it to Rogan. He put it to his lips and the fruity wine washed the ache out of his head. He kissed the girl's heavy breasts. They seemed to give off the fragrance of grapes; her whole body exuded the aroma of the wine, as if she herself were the very essence of it.

Rogan smiled at her. "And who are you?" he asked.

"I am Mrs. Genco Bari," she said. "But you may call me Lucia." At that moment there was a knock on the bolted door. She smiled at him. "And that is my husband come to reward you."

Lucia went to unbolt the door while Rogan reached to where his jacket hung on a chair, groping for his Walther pistol. Before he could find it the door swung open and Genco Bari came into the room. Behind his frail, wasted figure loomed two Sicilian peasants, shotguns cradled in their arms. One of the peasants was Tullio. He stared at Rogan impassively.

Genco Bari sat at his wife's dressing table. He smiled in a kindly way at Rogan. "Have no fear; I am not the typical, jealous Sicilian husband," he said. "As you see, it is obvious I can no longer fulfill my husbandly duties. I am a more worldly man than my fellow peasants, and so I permit my wife to satisfy her very natural needs. But never with someone from this village, and always with discretion. Last night I am afraid my poor Lucia became carried away by the new wine and her passion. But no matter. Here is your reward." He tossed a purse stuffed with money on the bed. Rogan did not move to take it.

Genco Bari turned to his wife. "Lucia, did he acquit himself well?"

Lucia flashed Rogan a brilliant smile and nodded. "Like a fine bull," she said mischievously.

Bari laughed, or rather he tried to laugh. But since there was no flesh on his face, it was merely a grimace of loose bones and skin and teeth. "You must forgive my wife," he said to Rogan. "She is a simple peasant girl with forthright, lusty ways. That is why I married her three years ago when I learned I was dying. I thought I could hold on to life by feasting on her body. But that soon ended. And then when I saw her suffering I broke all the traditions of our land. I permitted her to have lovers. But under conditions dictated by me, so that my honor and the honor of my family would remain untarnished. So let me warn you now: If you boast of this to anyone in Sicily, I will set my ferrets after you and you will never lie with women again."

Rogan said curtly, "I don't need that money, and I never tell stories about women."

Genco Bari stared at him intently. "There is something familiar about your face," he said. "And you speak Italian almost like a native. Have our paths ever crossed?"

"No," Rogan said. He was looking at Bari with pity. The man weighed no more than seventy pounds. His face was a skin-covered skull.

Genco Bari said musingly, as if talking to himself, "You were searching for me when you were in Palermo. Then the American agent Bailey set you on my trail. Tullio here"—he jerked his head at the armed guard—"tells me that at his wine booth you were inquiring where I lived and that I had invited you here. So we must know each other." He leaned toward Rogan. "Have you been sent here to kill me?" He smiled his ghastly smile. He flung out his arms jestingly. "You are too late," he said. "I am dying. There is no point in your killing me."

Rogan said quietly, "When you remember who I am, I'll answer that question."

Bari shrugged. "It doesn't matter," he said. "But until I do remember, I insist that you remain a guest here at my villa. Take a little holiday. You will amuse my wife, and perhaps you can spare an hour each day to chat with me.

I am always curious about America. I have many friends there. Say yes to my request; you won't be sorry for it."

Rogan nodded, then shook the hand outstretched to him. When Bari and his guards had left the bedroom Rogan asked Lucia, "How long does your husband have to live?"

Lucia shrugged. "Who knows? A month, a week, an hour. I feel sorry for him, but I am young; I have my life to live, so perhaps it is better for me if he dies soon. But I will weep for him. He is a very kind man. He has given my parents a farm, and he has promised to leave his whole estate to me when he dies. I would have gone without lovers. It was he who insisted. Now I am glad." She came and sat on Rogan's lap, ready for more of the same.

Rogan spent the next week at Genco Bari's villa. It became obvious that he could never hope to escape Sicily after he killed Bari. The Mafia organization would intercept him easily at the Palermo airport. His only hope was to kill Bari in such a way that his body would not be discovered for at least six hours. That would give him time to get on the plane.

He spent part of each day making plans and cultivating Bari. He found the Mafia Don extremely likeable, courteous, and helpful. They became almost good friends in that week. And although he went horseback riding and on amorous picnics with Lucia, he found his conversations with Genco Bari more entertaining. Lucia's sexual appetite and grape smell were overwhelming. It was with relief that Rogan settled down every evening to share Genco Bari's light supper and glass of grappa. Bari had changed completely from the murderer he had been ten years before. He treated Rogan like a son, and he was extremely interesting, especially when telling strange stories about the Mafia in Sicily.

"Do you know why no stone wall in Sicily is over two feet high?" he asked Rogan. "The government in Rome felt that too many Sicilians were ambushing each other from behind stone walls, so they thought that if they reduced the height of the walls they would reduce the number of murders. How foolish. Nothing will stop people from killing each other. Don't you agree?" And he gave Rogan a sharp look. Rogan merely smiled. He did not want to be led into any philosophical discussions about murder.

Bari told Rogan stories about the old Mafia feuds and protection rackets. How every branch of industry had its own Mafia branch clinging like a leech and sucking blood. That there was even a branch of the Mafia that collected protection money from young men who serenaded their ladies beneath their balconies. The whole island was unbelievably corrupt. But you could live in peace—if you, too, were a member of the Mafia.

Bari had become a farmer in 1946, because he had refused to have anything to do with the traffic in narcotics that sprang up after the war. "I was an evil man in those days," Genco Bari told Rogan with a deprecating smile. "I was violent. But I never harmed a woman, and I would never deal in narcotics. That is *infamità*. I always kept my honor. Even murderers and thieves have their honor."

Rogan smiled politely. Bari had forgotten about the

Munich Palace of Justice, and he had forgotten the screams of Christine preserved on the brown wax phonograph cylinder. It was time to remind him.

By the end of the week Rogan had thought of a plan that would let him kill Bari and make a clean getaway. He proposed to the Mafia Don that they both go for a picnic in Rogan's car. They would drive out into the country with a basket of food and jugs of wine and grappa and sit in the shade of a tree. The outing would do the ailing man good.

Bari smiled at Rogan. "That would be very fine. It is very thoughtful of you to waste your time on an old wreck like me. I'll give orders to have your car stocked with food and drink. Shall we take Lucia with us?"

Rogan frowned and shook his head. "She's too lively, and men can't talk with women around. I like your company too much to have it spoiled by a female's idle chatter." Bari laughed and they were agreed; they would leave early the next morning and return late in the evening. Genco Bari had some business in a few small villages that could be taken care of along the way. Rogan was glad to see that these villages were on the road to Palermo.

They started off the next morning with Rogan driving and Genco Bari, his skull-like face shielded by his inevitable cream-colored Panama hat, seated next to him. They drove a few hours on the main road to Palermo, and then Bari directed Rogan to take a side road that wound up in the hilly regions. The road ended in a narrow trail, and Rogan had to stop the car.

"Bring the food and wine," Genco Bari said. "We'll picnic beneath the rocks."

Rogan carried the basket to where Bari was standing in the shadow of the hill. There was a red-checked table-cloth to spread over the ground, and on top of that he put the covered dishes of fried aubergine, cold sausage, a loaf of crusty bread wrapped in a white napkin. There were wide short glasses for the wine, and Bari poured from the jug. When they had finished eating, Bari offered Rogan a long, thin black cigar. "Sicilian tobacco, rare, but the best in the world," Bari said. He flared his lighter and lit Rogan's cigar for him, then said in exactly the same tone of voice, "Why are you going to kill me today?"

Rogan, surprised, took a quick glance to see if he had been led into a trap. Genco Bari shook his head. "No, I have not taken any precautions to guard my life. It is of no value to me any longer. But I still like to satisfy my curiosity. Who are you and why do you wish to kill me?"

Rogan said slowly, "You told me once that you had never done violence to a woman. But you helped to kill my wife." Bari looked puzzled, so Rogan went on. "On *Rosenmontag*, 1945, in the Munich Palace of Justice. You fixed my tie before Eric Freisling shot me in the back of the head. But you never killed me. You never killed me. I stayed alive. The Freisling brothers are dead, Moltke and Pfann are dead. After I kill you I have only Pajerski and von Osteen to punish, and then I can die happy."

Genco Bari puffed on his cigar, stared at Rogan for a long time. "I knew you would have an honorable motive for killing me. You are so obviously an honorable man. All week I could see you planning how to kill me and then get safely on your plane in Palermo. So I've helped you. Leave my body here and go forward. Before anyone knows what has happened, you will be in Rome. Then I suggest you leave Italy as quickly as possible. The Mafia has a long arm."

"If you hadn't straightened my tie, if you hadn't distracted me so that Eric could sneak up behind me, I might not kill you," Rogan said.

On Bari's emaciated face was a look of surprise. Then he smiled sadly. "I never meant to trick you," he said. "I thought you knew you were going to die. And so I wanted you to feel a human touch, to comfort you in those last few moments without betraying myself to my fellow murderers. You see, I do not excuse myself from that deed. But I must insist to you now: I had nothing to do with your wife's death or with her screams."

The Sicilian sun was directly overhead and the rock overhanging them gave no shade. Rogan felt the sick anticipation rising in his stomach. "Was it von Osteen who killed her?" he said. "Tell me who tortured her, and I swear by her memory and her soul that I will let you go free."

Genco Bari stood up. For the first time in their relationship he was harsh and angry. "You fool," he said. "Haven't you realized I want you to kill me? You are my deliverer, not my executioner. Every day I suffer terrible pain that no drugs can completely banish. The cancer is in every cell of my body, but it can't kill me. As we did not succeed in killing you in the Munich Palace of Justice. I may live in this pain for years to come, cursing God. I knew from the very first day that you wanted to kill me. I helped you in every way to find an opportunity." He smiled at Rogan. "This sounds like a rather grim joke, but

I will only tell you the truth about your wife if you promise to kill me."

Rogan said harshly, "Why don't *you* just kill yourself?"

He was surprised when Genco Bari bowed his head, then raised it to look directly into his eyes. Almost with shame, the Italian whispered, "It would be a mortal sin. I believe in God."

There was a long silence. They were both standing. Finally Rogan said, "Tell me if it was von Osteen who killed my wife, and I promise to end yours."

Genco Bari spoke slowly. "It was the leader of our group, Klaus von Osteen, who had the screams recorded to torture you with later. He was a strange, terrible man— no other man I have ever known would have thought of such a thing at such a time. For it wasn't planned, you know. It was all an accident. So he had to think of the recording right there, right on the spur of the moment, as the girl was dying."

Rogan said hoarsely, "Then who tortured her? Who killed her?"

Genco Bari looked directly into his eyes and said gravely, "You did."

Rogan felt the blood pounding in his head, the skull around the silver plate throbbing with pain. He said thickly, "You lousy bastard, you tricked me. You're not going to tell me who did it." He took the Walther pistol from his jacket and pointed it at Bari's stomach. "Tell me who killed my wife."

Again Genco Bari looked directly into Rogan's eyes and said gravely, "You did. She died giving birth to a dead child. None of us touched her. We were sure she knew nothing. But von Osteen recorded her screams to frighten you with."

"You're lying," Rogan said. Without even thinking he pulled the trigger of the Walther pistol. The report echoed against the rocks like thunder, and Genco Bari's frail form was hurled to the ground almost five feet from where he had been standing. Rogan walked to where the dying man was crumpled against a rock. He put the pistol against Bari's ear.

The dying man opened his eyes and nodded gratefully; he whispered to Rogan, "Don't blame yourself. Her screams were terrible because all pain, all death, is equally terrible. You too must die again, and it will not be less terrible." His breath was coming in bloody ribbons of spit. "Forgive me, as I forgive you," he said.

Rogan held the man in his arms, not firing again, waiting for him to die. It took only a few minutes, and he had plenty of time to catch his plane in Palermo. But before he left he covered Genco Bari's body with a blanket from the car. He hoped it would be found soon.

CHAPTER 13

At Rome Rogan caught a flight to Budapest. Arthur Bailey had kept his promise and the visas were waiting for him. Rogan took along some whiskey and stayed drunk on the plane. He couldn't forget what Genco Bari had told him: that Christine had died in childbirth; that he, Rogan, had been responsible for her death. But could a death so common to women since time began cause the terrible screams of pain he had heard on the phonograph in the Munich Palace of Justice? And that cruel bastard von Osteen making the record. Only a genius of evil could think of something so inhuman on the spur of the moment. Rogan forgot his own feelings of guilt for a moment as he thought of killing von Osteen and the pleasure it would give him. He thought of letting Pajerski's execution wait, but he was already on the plane bound for Hungary; Arthur Bailey had already arranged things for him in Budapest. Rogan smiled grimly. He knew something Bailey didn't know.

In Budapest, more than a little drunk, Rogan went directly to the United States consulate and asked to see the interpreter. This was all according to Arthur Bailey's instructions.

A small nervous man with a toothbrush mustache led him to the inner chambers. "I am the interpreter," he said. "Who sent you to me?"

"A mutual friend named Arthur Bailey," Rogan told him.

The little man ducked away into another room. After a few moments he came back and said in a frightened, timid voice, "Please follow me, sir. I will take you to someone who will help you."

They entered a room in which a burly man with thinning hair waited for them. He shook Rogan's hand with vigor and introduced himself as Stefan Vrostk. "I am the one who will aid you in your mission," he said. "Our friend Bailey has requested I give it my personal attention." With a wave of his hand he dismissed the little interpreter.

When they were alone in the room, Vrostk began to speak in an arrogant manner. "I have read about your case. I have been briefed on what you have done. I have been informed on your future plans." He spoke as if he were a man of great importance; he was, obviously, a man of overwhelming conceit.

Rogan sat back and just listened. Vrostk went on. "You must understand that here behind the Iron Curtain things are very different. You cannot hope to operate so flagrantly as you have done. Your record as an agent in World War II does show you are prone to carelessness.

Your network was destroyed because you did not take proper precautions when you used your clandestine radio. Isn't that true?" He gave Rogan a patronizing smile. But Rogan continued to look at him impassively.

Vrostk was a little nervous now, but this did not lessen his arrogance one bit. "I will point out Pajerski to you—where he works, his living habits, how he is guarded. The actual execution you must do yourself. I will then arrange to have the underground spirit you out of the country. But let me impress upon you that you are to do nothing without consulting me. You will do nothing without my approval. And you must accept without questioning my plans for your escape from this country once you have completed your mission. Do you understand this?"

Rogan could feel the anger mounting to his head. "Sure," he said. "I understand. I understand everything perfectly. You work for Bailey, don't you?"

"Yes," Vrostk said.

Rogan smiled. "OK, then I'll follow your orders. I'll tell you everything before I do it." He laughed. "Now show me where I can get my hands on Pajerski."

Vrostk smiled paternally. "First we must have you checked into a hotel where you will be safe. Take a little nap, and this evening you and I shall dine at the Café Black Violin. And there you shall see Pajerski. He dines there every evening, plays chess there, meets his friends there. It is his hangout, as you say in America."

In the small side-street hotel Vrostk had found for him, Rogan sat in a stuffed chair and made his own plans. In doing so he thought about Wenta Pajerski and everything the raw-boned Hungarian had done to him in the Munich Palace of Justice.

The face was huge, red, and warty as a hog's, yet Pajerski had been only casual in his cruelty, and sometimes he had been kind. He had halted the interrogation to give Rogan a drink of water or a cigarette, slipped mint wafers into his hand. And though Rogan knew that Pajerski was deliberately playing the role of the "good guy," the classic "nice cop" who makes some prisoners talk where nothing else will, he could not even now help feeling the glow of gratitude the act of kindness in itself inspired.

Whatever the motive, the sugary mints had been real, the sweet bits of chocolate broke his suffering. The water and cigarettes were miraculous gifts of life. They lived. They entered his body. So why not let Pajerski live? He remembered the hulking man's vitality, his obvious joy in the good things of life that were material. The physical pleasure he took in eating, drinking, and even in the tortures demanded by the interrogation. But he had laughed when Eric Freisling was creeping up behind Rogan to fire the bullet into his skull. Pajerski had enjoyed that.

Rogan remembered something else. On the afternoon of the first interrogation in the Munich Palace of Justice, they had played the recording of Christine's screams from the next room. Rogan had twisted and cried out in agony. Pajerski had sauntered out of the high-domed room saying jokingly to Rogan, "Be at ease; I go to make your wife scream with pleasure instead of pain."

Rogan sighed. They had all played their parts so well. They had succeeded in tricking him every time. They had failed in only one thing: They had not killed him. And now it was his turn. It was his turn to materialize suddenly out of the darkness, bearing torture and death in his hands. It was his turn to know and see everything, and their turn to guess and fear what would happen next.

CHAPTER 14

That night Rogan went with Stefan Vrostk to the Black Violin. It proved to be exactly the kind of place he would have imagined as being Wenta Pajerski's favorite hangout. The food was good and the plates were heaped high. The drinks were strong and cheap. The waitresses were handsomely buxom, cheerful, lusty, and had a dozen sly ways of presenting their plump bottoms to be pinched. The accordion music was bouncy, and the atmosphere was hazy with pungent tobacco smoke.

Wenta Pajerski entered at exactly 7:00 p.m. He had not changed at all, just as animals never look older after maturity, until they reach an extreme age. And Wenta Pajerski was an animal. He pinched the first waitress so hard she let out a little scream of pain. He drank a huge tankard of beer in one slug, choking it down in his refusal to stop and draw a breath. Then he sat at a large round table, reserved for him, and was soon joined by male cronies. They laughed and joked and drank French cognac by the bottle. Meanwhile a blond waitress brought an oblong carved chest to the table. With great relish, Pajerski opened it up and took out chess pieces. The chest itself opened up into a chessboard. Pajerski appropriated the white pieces for himself, with their advantage of moving first, without giving his opponent the usual hidden choice between black and white. This was an insight into the giant Hungarian's character. He had not changed.

Rogan and Vrostk watched Pajerski's table all evening. Pajerski played chess until nine, drinking all the while. At exactly nine the blond waitress took away the chess set and brought dinner to the table.

Pajerski ate with such animal gusto that Rogan felt almost sorry he had to be killed. It was like killing some happy-go-lucky unreasoning animal. Pajerski lifted the soup bowl to his lips to lap up the last dregs. He used a huge spoon, instead of a fork, to shovel mountains of gravy-soaked rice into his cavernous mouth. He drank his wine from the bottle, with an impatient gurgling thirst. Then he let out a wave of belches that rolled across the room.

When he was finished, Pajerski paid for everyone's dinner, pinched the waitress' behind, and shoved a huge tip of crumpled paper money down inside her dress so that he could squeeze her breast. Everybody put up with his behavior; they were obviously either very fond of him or very afraid of him. His male companions followed him out onto the dark streets, marching arm in arm, talking loudly. When they passed an open café whose music rolled out into the open, Wenta Pajerski did a bearlike waltz down the street, whirling his nearest companion in his arms.

Rogan and Vrostk followed them until they disappeared into an ornately faced building. Then Vrostk hailed a cab, and they drove to the consulate. Vrostk gave Rogan the Hungarian's dossier to read. "This will fill you in on the rest of Pajerski's evening," he said. "We won't have to follow him everywhere. He does the same thing every night."

The dossier was short but informative. Wenta Pajerski was the executive officer of the Communist secret police in Budapest. He worked hard all day in the town hall administration building. He also had his living quarters in this building. Both office and living quarters were heavily guarded by special details of the secret police. He always left the building punctually at 6:30 p.m., but was escorted by guards in plain clothes. At least two official guards were among the men who walked down the street with him.

Wenta Pajerski was the only one of the seven torturers who had remained in the same kind of work. Ordinary citizens suspected of activities against the State disappeared into his office and were never seen again. He was believed responsible for the kidnapping of West German scientists. Pajerski was high on the list of Cold War criminals the West would like to see liquidated. Rogan smiled grimly. He understood Bailey's cooperation and why Vrostk was so anxious that everything be checked out with him. The repercussions of Pajerski's murder would shake the whole city of Budapest.

The dossier also explained the ornate building Pajerski had entered with his friends. It was the most expensive and exclusive brothel, not only in Budapest but in the whole area behind the Iron Curtain as well. After caressing every girl in the parlor, Pajerski never took fewer than two upstairs for his pleasure. An hour later he would reappear in the street, puffing on an enormous cigar, looking as content as a bear ready to hibernate. But both inside the house and out, his guards stuck as close to him as possible, without interfering with his pleasures. He was not vulnerable in that area.

Rogan closed the dossier and looked up at Vrostk. "How long has your organization been trying to kill him?" he asked.

Vrostk grimaced. "What makes you think that?"

Rogan said, "Everything in this dossier. Earlier today you gave me a lot of crap about how you're the big boss of this operation because you're so much better an agent than I am. I took it. But you're not my boss. I'll tell you what you have to know, and I'll count on you to get me out of the country after I kill Pajerski. But that's all. And I'll give you some good advice: Don't pull any fast ones on me—none of those tricky Intelligence moves. I'd kill you as soon as I'd kill Pajerski. Sooner. I like him better." Rogan gave the man a brutally cold smile.

Stefan Vrostk flushed. "I didn't mean to offend you earlier," he said. "I meant it well."

Rogan shrugged. "I haven't come all this way to be jerked around like a puppet. I'll pull your chestnuts out of the fire; I'll kill Pajerski for you. But don't ever try to bull me again." He got out of his chair and walked out the door. Vrostk followed him and conducted him out of the consulate, then held out his hand. Rogan ignored it and walked away.

He could not explain why he had got so tough with

Vrostk. Perhaps it was the feeling that only an accident of time and history had prevented Vrostk from being one of the seven men in the high-domed room of the Munich Palace of Justice. But it was also that he distrusted Vrostk even now. Anyone who acted so imperiously in small matters had to be weak.

Not trusting anyone else, Rogan checked out the dossier by personal observation. For six days he frequented the Café Black Violin and memorized Pajerski's every move. The dossier proved to be correct in every particular. But Rogan noticed something that was not in the dossier. Pajerski, like many genial giants, always looked for an advantage. For example, he always took the white pieces, without fail, in his chess games. He had a nervous habit of scratching his chin with the pointed crown of his king piece. Rogan also noted that though the chess set was the property of the Black Violin, it was not loaned to other patrons until Pajerski had finished with it for the evening.

The Hungarian also passed a café whose music delighted him, and he would invariably go into his bearlike dance when he heard the music from that café. The dance took him usually thirty yards ahead of his guards to a street corner, which he then turned. For perhaps one minute he was out of the guards' sight, alone and vulnerable. Vrostk wasn't such a hot agent, Rogan thought, not if that one vulnerable minute was not recorded in the dossier. Unless it had been deliberately omitted.

Rogan kept checking. He thought the brothel a likely place to catch Pajerski unguarded. But he found that two men from the secret police invariably took their posts outside the bedroom door while Pajerski took his exercise within.

The problem was admittedly difficult. Pajerski's living and working quarters were impregnable. Only in the evening was he slightly vulnerable. When he danced around that corner there would be a minute to kill him and escape. But a minute would not be enough to evade the guards following. In his mind Rogan kept reviewing Pajerski's every move, searching for a fatal chink in the man's security armor. On the sixth night he fell asleep with the problem still unsolved. What made it even more difficult was that Pajerski had to know why he was being killed before he died. For Rogan this was essential.

In the middle of the night he woke up. He had had a dream in which he played chess with Wenta Pajerski, and Pajerski kept saying to him, "You stupid Amerikaner, you have had a checkmate for three moves." And Rogan had kept staring at the board looking for the elusive winning move, staring at the huge white king carved out of wood. Smiling slyly, Pajerski picked up the white king and used its pointed crown to scratch his chin. It was a hint. Rogan sat up in bed. The dream had given him his answer. He knew how he would kill Pajerski.

The next day he went to the consulate and asked to see Vrostk. When he told the agent what tools and other equipment he would need Vrostk looked at him in astonishment, but Rogan refused to explain. Vrostk told him it would take at least the rest of the day to get everything together. Rogan nodded. "I'll come by tomorrow morning to pick it up. Tomorrow night your friend Pajerski will be dead."

CHAPTER 15

I n Munich every day was the same for Rosalie. She had settled into the pension to wait for Rogan's return. She checked the Munich airport schedules and found that there was a daily flight from Budapest, arriving at 10:00 p.m. After that, every night she waited at the gate to check the passengers coming off the Budapest plane. She sensed that Rogan might not come back to her, that he would not want her involved in his murder of von Osteen. But since he was the only man, the only human being she cared about, she went every evening to the airport. She prayed that he had not died in Sicily; and then as time went on, she prayed that he had not died in Budapest. But it didn't matter. She was prepared to make her evening pilgrimage for the rest of her life.

During the second week she went shopping in the central square of Munich. That was where the Palace of Justice was situated. It had miraculously escaped damage during the war and now housed the criminal courts of the city. Nazi concentration camp commandants and guards were being tried for their war crimes in those courtrooms at almost every session.

On an impulse, Rosalie went into the massive building. In the cool, dark hall she studied the public bulletin boards to see if von Osteen was sitting as judge that day. He was not. Then a little notice caught her eye. The municipal court system was advertising for a nurse's aide to work in the emergency hospital room of the court.

Again on an impulse, Rosalie applied for the position. Her training in the asylum had given her the necessary basic skills, and she was immediately taken on. There was a great shortage of medical personnel in all postwar German cities.

The emergency hospital room was in the basement of the Municipal Palace of Justice. It had its own private entrance, a small door that led into the huge inner courtyard. With a shock of horror, Rosalie realized that it was in this courtyard that the wounded Rogan had been thrown onto a pile of corpses.

The emergency room was astonishingly busy. Wives of convicted criminals sentenced to long terms in prison collapsed and were brought down to be revived. Elderly swindlers on trial suffered heart attacks. Rosalie's duties were more clerical than medical. She had to record every case in a huge blue book on the admittance desk. The young doctor on duty was immediately taken by her beauty and asked her to dinner. She refused him with a polite smile. Some of the sleek attorneys accompanying their sick clients to the medical room asked her if she would be interested in working in their offices. She smiled at them and politely said she would not.

She was interested in only one man in the Munich Palace of Justice: Klaus von Osteen. When he sat in court she attended the trial by taking a very late lunch hour and skipping lunch.

He was not the man she had imagined. He had a dignified ugliness, but his voice was kind and gentle. He treated accused criminals with the utmost courtesy and a trace of genuine, merciful pity. She heard him sentence a man found guilty of a particularly violent and sadistic crime, and he had not indulged in the usual righteousness of a judge meting out punishment. He had let the convicted man keep his dignity.

One day she found herself directly behind him on a street near the Munich Palace of Justice, and she trailed him as he limped down the street. One of his legs was shorter than the other. He was accompanied by a detective guard who moved a few steps behind him and seemed very alert. But von Osteen himself seemed preoccupied. Despite this preoccupation, he was extraordinarily courteous to people who greeted him in the street and to the chauffeur of the official car that was assigned him.

Rosalie noticed that the man had an extraordinary magnetism. The respect shown him by his fellow judges, the clerks of the court, and the lawyers testified to von Osteen's force of character. And when a woman laden with bundles collided with him in the street, von Osteen helped her to pick up her bundles, though he was grimacing with pain. He did it with genuine courtliness. It was hard to believe that this was the man Rogan hated so much.

Rosalie found out as much as she could about von Osteen so that she would have the information for Rogan when he arrived in Munich. She learned that von Osteen had a wife who was a power in the social life of Munich and an aristocrat in her own right. She was much younger than von Osteen. They did not have any children. She learned that von Osteen had more political control of the city than any other official, including the *Bürgermeister*. He was also backed by the U.S. State Department officials as a proven democrat, both anti-Nazi and anti-Communist.

Despite all this, it was enough for her to know that Rogan hated the man to make all von Osteen's virtues count for nothing. She kept a notebook on von Osteen's habits, to make it easier for Rogan to kill him.

And every night at 10:00 she waited at the airport for the flight from Budapest, certain that Rogan would return.

CHAPTER 16

When Rogan woke up on his final day in Budapest, his first act was to destroy the dossiers he had compiled on the seven men. Then he went through his belongings to see if there was anything he wanted to keep. But there was nothing except his passport.

He packed everything else and carried his bags to the railway station. He checked the bags into an empty coin locker, then left the station. Crossing over one of the many bridges in the city, he casually dropped the locker key into the river. Then he went to the consulate.

Vrostk had gathered everything he needed. Rogan checked the items—the small jeweler's drill and chipping tools, the tiny wires, the timing device, the liquid explosive, and some special electronic parts of tiny size. Rogan smiled and said, "Very good."

Vrostk preened himself. "I have a very efficient organization. It was not easy to get all these things on such short notice."

"To show my appreciation," Rogan said, "I'm going to buy you a late breakfast at the Café Black Violin. Then we'll come back here and I'll go to work with this stuff. And I'll also tell you what I'm going to do."

At the café they ordered coffee and brioches. Then, to Vrostk's obvious surprise, Rogan called for the chess set. The waitress brought it over, and Rogan set up the pieces, taking the whites for himself.

Vrostk said in an annoyed voice, "I have no time for such foolishness. I must get back to my office."

"Play," Rogan said. Something in his voice made Vrostk suddenly quiet. He let Rogan make the first move and then moved his black pawn. The game was soon over. He beat Rogan easily and the pieces were dumped back into the set for the waitress to carry away. Rogan gave a large tip. Outside the café he hailed a taxi to take them back to the consulate. He was in a hurry now; every moment was valuable.

In Vrostk's office Rogan sat down at the table that had the special equipment on it.

Vrostk was angry; it was the bullying anger of a small-minded man. "What is the meaning of all this foolishness?" he asked. "I demand to know."

Rogan put his right hand into his jacket pocket, pulled it out again clenched. He thrust it at Vrostk and then opened it. Lying in his palm was the white king.

Rogan worked intently at the table for nearly three hours. He drilled a hole in the bottom of the king, and then took the bottom out entirely. Working very carefully, he hollowed out the inside of the chess piece and packed it with liquid explosive, wires, and the tiny electronic parts. When he was finished he put the bottom back on, and then with buffing cloth and enamel he hid all scratches and chips. He held the chess piece in his hand, trying to see if the extra weight was too obvious. He did notice a little difference, but he reasoned that this was because he was looking for the difference. The piece would pass.

He turned to Vrostk. "At eight o'clock tonight this thing will blow up in Pajerski's face. I've got it fixed so that nobody else will get hurt. There's just enough to kill the man holding the piece. And Pajerski always scratches his chin with it. That and the timing device will set off the explosive. If I see someone else holding it, I'll interfere and deactivate it. But I've watched Pajerski, and I'm sure he'll be the guy who'll have the piece in his hand at eight tonight. Now I want you to have your underground people pick me up at the corner two blocks from the café. I'm counting on your organization to get me out of the country."

"You mean you're going to stay in the café until Pajerski is killed?" Vrostk asked. "That's sheer madness. Why not leave beforehand?"

"I want to make sure nobody else gets killed," Rogan said. "And before he dies, I also want Pajerski to know who killed him and why, and I can't do that unless I'm there."

Vrostk shrugged. "It's your affair. As for my people picking you up two blocks from the café, that's too dangerous for them. I'll have a black Mercedes limousine waiting for you in front of the consulate here. It will be flying the consulate flag. What time do you want it to be ready?"

Rogan frowned. "I may change the timing on the explosive, or it may possibly go off ahead of time if Pajerski keeps scratching his chin with it too much. Better have the car waiting for me at seven thirty and tell them to expect me at ten minutes past eight. I'll be on foot, and I'll just get into the car without any fuss. I assume they know me by sight. You've shown me to them?"

Vrostk smiled. "Of course. Now I suppose you and I will have a late lunch and a game of chess at the Black Violin so that you can return the white king."

Rogan smiled. "You're getting smarter all the time."

Over coffee they played the second game of chess, and Rogan won easily. When they left the café, the booby-trapped white king was safely back with its fellow chess pieces.

That evening Rogan left his small hotel room at exactly 6:00. The Walther pistol was tucked under his arm and buttoned securely into its holster. The silencer was in his left jacket pocket. His passport and visas were in his inside jacket pocket. He walked slowly and leisurely to the Café Black Violin and took his usual small corner table. He unfolded a newspaper, ordered a bottle of Tokay, and told the waitress he would order food later.

He had drunk half the bottle when Wenta Pajerski came roaring into the café. Rogan looked at his watch. The giant Hungarian was right on schedule; it was 7:00 p.m. He watched Pajerski pinch the blond waitress, yell to his waiting friends, and have his first drink. It was about time for him to call for his chess set, but he ordered a second drink. Rogan felt himself go tense. Would this be the first night that Pajerski would pass up his chess games? For some reason it seemed to have slipped his mind this evening. But then, without his calling for it, the waitress brought the chess set to Pajerski's table, waiting expectantly for the pinch that would reward her fore-thought.

It almost looked as if Pajerski would wave her away. But then he grinned, his warty piggy face becoming a mass of joviality. He pinched the blond waitress so hard that she gave a little scream of pain.

Rogan called to the waitress and asked her for a pencil and a piece of notepaper. He looked at his watch. It read 7:30. On the rough brown notepaper he wrote: "I will turn your screams of pleasure into pain. *Rosenmontag*, 1945, in the Munich Palace of Justice."

He waited until his watch read 7:55; then he called a waitress over and handed her the note. "Give this to Mr. Pajerski," he said. "Then come right back to me and I will give you this." He showed her a banknote that was more than her weekly salary. He didn't want her standing near Pajerski when the booby trap went off.

Pajerski was scratching his chin with the white king when the waitress handed him the note. He read it slowly, translating the English audibly, his lips moving. He raised his eyes to stare directly at Rogan. Rogan stared back at him, smiling slightly. His watch read 7:59. And then as he saw the recognition slowly dawn in Pajerski's eyes the white king exploded.

The explosion was deafening. Pajerski had been holding the chess piece in his right hand under his chin. Rogan had been staring into his eyes. Then suddenly Pajerski's eyes disappeared in the explosion, and Rogan found himself staring into two empty bloody sockets. Pieces of flesh and bone spattered all over the room, and then Pajerski's head, its flesh shredded, slumped over on flaps of skin that were still holding the neck to the body. Rogan slipped out of his seat and left the café by the kitchen door. The screaming, stampeding crowd took no notice of him.

Out on the street he walked one block to a main avenue and hailed a taxi. "To the airport," he told the driver; then, just to make sure, he said, "Take the street that goes past the American consulate."

He could hear the whine of police car sirens speeding to the Café Black Violin. In a few minutes his taxi was on the broad avenue that led past the consulate. "Don't go so fast," he told the driver. He leaned back so that he could not be seen from the street.

There was no Mercedes limousine waiting there. The street was empty of all vehicles, which was in itself unusual. But it had a hell of a lot of pedestrians, waiting to cross at corners and window-shopping. And most of the pedestrians were big, burly men. To Rogan's experienced eye they had secret police written all over them. "Speed it up to the airport," he told the driver.

It was then that he noticed what seemed like a physical coldness in his chest. It was as if his whole body were being touched by death. He felt the chilliness spread. But he was not cold. He did not feel any real physical discomfort. It was simply as if he himself had become some sort of host to death.

He had no trouble getting on the plane. His visa was in order, and there was no sign of any special police activity at the airport. His heart beat swiftly when he boarded the aircraft, but again there were no complications. The plane took off, climbed, and then it leveled off and headed for the German border and Munich.

That night Rosalie left her job as nurse's aide in the Munich Palace of Justice at 6:00 p.m. The young doctor who worked with her insisted she have dinner with him. Afraid of losing her job, she agreed. He made sure the meal took a long time by ordering several courses. It was after 9:00 p.m. when they finished. Rosalie looked at her watch. "You must excuse me; I have an important engagement at ten," she said, and started to gather up her coat and gloves.

The young doctor had a disappointed look on his face. It did not occur to Rosalie that she could miss meeting the plane one night and keep her escort company for the rest of the evening. If she missed meeting the Budapest plane even one time, it would mean she thought Rogan was dead. She walked out of the restaurant and hailed a taxi. By the time she got to the airport, it was nearly 10:00. By the time she ran through the terminal to the Budapest plane arrival gate, passengers were already coming out. Out of habit, she lit a cigarette as she watched them. And then she saw Rogan and her heart nearly broke.

He looked dreadfully ill. His eyes were sunken, the muscles of his face were rigid, and there was a fearful stiffness in his body movements. He had not seen her, and she started running toward him, calling his name through her sobs.

Rogan heard the clicking of a woman's heels on marble, heard Rosalie calling his name. He started to turn away, then turned back to catch her as she rushed into his arms. And then he was kissing her wet face and her lovely eyes as she whispered, "I'm so happy, I'm so happy. I came here every night, and every night I thought you might have died and I'd never know and I'd be coming here for the rest of my life."

Holding her close, feeling her warmth, Rogan felt the icy chill that had been part of his body begin to melt away, as if he were coming alive again. He knew then that he would have to keep her with him.

CHAPTER 17

They took a taxi to the pension, and Rosalie led Rogan up to the room she'd had while she was alone in Munich. It was a comfortable place, half bedroom, half living room, with a small green sofa curved into its middle. There was a vase of wilted roses on the table; some of their scent still hung in the air. Rogan reached out for Rosalie as soon as they had locked the door behind them. They quickly undressed and went to bed, but their lovemaking was too frantic, too filled with tension.

They smoked a cigarette together in the darkness, and then Rosalie began to weep. "Why can't you stop now?" she whispered. "Why can't you just stop?"

Rogan didn't answer. He knew what she meant. That if he let Klaus von Osteen go free, his life, and hers, could start again. They would stay alive. If he went after von Osteen the chances of his escaping were small. Rogan sighed. He could never tell another human being what von Osteen had done to him in the Munich Palace of Justice; it was too shameful. Shameful in the same way that their attempt to kill him had been shameful. He knew only one thing! He could never live on earth as long as von Osteen was alive. He could never sleep a night through without nightmares as long as von Osteen was alive. To balance his own private world he had to kill the seventh and last man.

And yet, in a strange way, he dreaded the moment when he would see von Osteen again. He had to remind himself that now von Osteen would be the victim, von Osteen would shriek with fear, von Osteen would collapse in terror. But it was hard to imagine all this. For back in those terrible days when the seven men had tortured him in the Munich Palace of Justice, in those nightmare days when Christine's screams from the next room had set his body trembling with anguish, Rogan had come to regard Klaus von Osteen finally as God, had almost come fearfully to love him.

Rosalie had fallen sleep, her face still wet with tears. Rogan lit another cigarette. His mind, his invincible memory, and all the agonies of remembrance imprisoned him once again in the high-domed room of the Munich Palace of Justice.

In the early morning hours the jail guards would come into his cell with small rubber clubs and a battered tin bucket for his vomit. They would use the rubber clubs to beat his stomach, his thighs, his groin. Pinned helplessly against the iron bars of his cell, Rogan felt the black bile gush into his mouth, and he'd retch. One of the guards would skillfully catch the vomit in the tin bucket. They never asked any questions. They beat him automatically, just to set the proper tone for the day.

Another guard wheeled in a breakfast tray on which stood a chunk of black bread and a bowl of grayish, lumpy gruel they called oatmeal. They made Rogan eat, and since he was always hungry, he gobbled the oatmeal and gnawed at the bread, which was rubbery stale. After he had eaten, the guards would stand around in a circle as if they were going to beat him again. Rogan's physical fear, his body organs weakened by malnutrition and torture, made it impossible for him to control his bowels at this moment. They opened against his will: He could feel the seat of his pants becoming sticky as the oatmeal oozed out of him.

As the foul stench filled the cell the guards dragged him out of his prison and through the halls of the Munich Palace of Justice. The marble halls were deserted this early in the morning, but Rogan would be ashamed of the trail of the tiny brown dots he left behind him. His bowels were still open, and though he keyed up all his nervous energy to close them, he could feel both pant legs go damp. The stench followed him down the halls. But now the swelling bruises on his body blotted out his shame until he had to sit down before his seven interrogators, and then the sticky mess plastered against the length of his lower back.

The guards shackled his arms and legs to a heavy wooden chair and put the keys on the long mahogany table. As soon as one of the seven interrogators arrived to begin the day's work, the guards left. Then the other members of the interrogation team would saunter in, some of them holding their breakfast coffee cups in their hands. During the first week, Klaus von Osteen always arrived last. This was the week that "normal" physical torture was used on Rogan.

Because of the complicated nature of the information Rogan had to give, the intricate codes and the mental energy required to recall his memorized digital patterns, physical torture proved to be too shattering to the thought process. After torture Rogan could not have given them the codes even if he had wanted to. It was Klaus von Osteen who first understood this and ordered all physical persuasion held to a "gentle" minimum. Afterward von Osteen was always the first member of the interrogation team to arrive in the morning.

In the early morning hours, von Osteen's beautifully chiseled aristocratic face was pale with shaving talcum, his eyes still gentle with sleep. Older than Rogan by a generation, he was the father every young man would like to have: distinguished-looking, without being foppish; sincere, without being oily or unctuous; grave, yet with a touch of humor; fair, yet stern. And in the weeks that followed, Rogan, worn down by physical fatigue, lack of proper food and rest, the constant torturing of his nerves, came to feel about von Osteen as if he were a protective father figure who was punishing him for his own good. His intellect rejected this attitude as ridiculous. The man was the chief of his torturers, responsible for all his pain. And yet emotionally, schizophrenically, he waited for von Osteen each morning as a child awaits his father.

The first morning von Osteen arrived before the others he put a cigarette in Rogan's mouth and lit it. Then he spoke, not questioning, but explaining his own position.

He, von Osteen, was doing his duty for the Fatherland by interrogating Rogan. Rogan was not to think it was a personal thing. He had an affection for Rogan. Rogan was almost young enough to be the son he never had. It distressed him that Rogan was being stubborn. What possible purpose could such childish defiance have? The secret codes in Rogan's brain would no longer be used by the Allies, that was certain. A sufficient time had elapsed to render useless any information he gave them. Why could not Rogan end this foolishness and save them all suffering? For the torturers suffered with the tortured. Did he think they did not?

Then he reassured Rogan. The questioning would end. The war would end. Rogan and his wife Christine would be together again and happy again. The fever of war and murder would be over, and human beings would not have to fear each other any longer. Rogan was not to despair. And von Osteen would pat Rogan's shoulder comfortingly.

But when the other interrogators sauntered into the room von Osteen's manner would change. Again he became the chief interrogator. His deep-set eyes bored into Rogan's eyes. His melodious voice became harsh, strident. Yet curiously enough it was the harshness of a strict father with a note of love for his wayward child. There was something so magnetic, so powerful in von Osteen's personality that Rogan believed the role von Osteen played: that the interrogation was just; that he, Rogan, had brought the physical pain upon himself.

Then had come the days when he heard Christine's screams from the next room. On those days von Osteen had not arrived early in the morning, had always arrived last. And then there was that terrible day when they had let him into the next room and showed him the phonograph and the spinning record that preserved Christine's agony. Von Osteen had said smilingly, "She died on the first day of torture. We've tricked you." And Rogan, hating him at that moment with such intensity, had become ill, bile spilling out of his mouth onto his prison clothing.

Von Osteen had lied even then. Genco Bari said that Christine had died during childbirth, and Rogan believed Bari. But why did von Osteen lie? Why did he wish his people to seem more evil than they actually were? And then Rogan, remembering, realized the brilliant psychology behind von Osteen's every word and deed.

The hatred he felt for those who had killed his wife had made him want to stay alive. He wanted to stay alive so that he could kill them all and smile down at their own tortured bodies. And it was this hatred, this hope for revenge, that had crumbled his resistance and in the following months made him start giving his interrogators all the secret codes he could remember.

Von Osteen started coming early again, the first one in the interrogation room. Again he began to console Rogan, his voice magnetic with understanding. After the first few days he always unshackled Rogan's arms and legs and brought him coffee and cigarettes for breakfast. He kept assuring Rogan that he would be set free as soon as the codes were completed. And then one morning he came in very early, closed and locked the door of the high-domed room behind him, and said to Rogan, "I must tell you a secret which you must promise not to reveal." Rogan nodded. Von Osteen, his face grave and friendly, said, "Your wife is still alive. Yesterday she gave birth to a baby boy. They are both doing well, they are both being well cared for. And I give you my solemn word of honor that the three of you will be united when you have finished giving us all the information we need. But you must not breathe a word of this to the others. They may cause trouble, since I am exceeding the bounds of my authority by making you this promise."

Rogan was stunned. He searched von Osteen's face to see if the man was lying. But there was no doubting the kind sincerity in the German's eyes, the gentle goodness that seemed to be the very essence of his facial bones. Rogan believed. And the thought that Christine was alive, that he would see her beautiful face again, that he would hold her soft slender body in his arms again, that she was not dead and under the earth—all this made him break down and weep. Von Osteen patted him on the shoulder, saying softly in his hypnotic voice, "I know, I know. I am sorry I could not tell you sooner. It was all a trick, you see, part of my job. But now it's no longer necessary and I wanted to make you happy."

He made Rogan dry his tears, and then he unlocked the door to the interrogation room. The other six men were waiting outside, coffee cups in their hands. They seemed angry at being shut out, angry that their leader was in some way allied to their victim.

That night in his cell Rogan dreamed of Christine and the baby son he had never seen. Oddly enough the baby's face was very clear in his dream, fat and pink-cheeked, but Christine's face was hidden in shadows.

When he called to her she came out of the shadows, and he could see her, see that she was happy. He dreamed of them every night.

Five days later it was *Rosenmontag*, and when von Osteen came into the room he was carrying an armful of civilian clothing. He smiled a genuinely happy smile and said to Rogan, "Today is the day I keep my promise to you." And then the other six men crowded into the room. They congratulated Rogan as if they were professors who had helped him graduate from school with honors. Rogan started putting on the clothes. Genco Bari helped to knot his tie, but Rogan kept his eyes on von Osteen, asking a mute question with his eyes, asking if he would see his wife and child. And von Osteen understood and nodded his head, secretively, reassuringly. Someone clapped the fedora on Rogan's head.

As he stood there looking at their smiling faces he realized one of them was missing. Then he felt the cold muzzle of the gun against the back of his neck and the hat tilted forward over his eyes. In that one-millionth of a second he understood everything and sent a last despairing look at von Osteen, crying out in his mind, "Father, Father, I believed. Father, I forgave all your torture, your treachery. I forgive you for murdering my wife and giving me hope. Save me now. Save me now." And the last thing he saw before the back of his skull exploded was von Osteen's gentle face contorting into a devil's mocking laugh.

Now lying in bed beside Rosalie, Rogan knew that killing von Osteen just once would not be enough to satisfy him. There should be a way of bringing him back to life and killing him over and over again. For von Osteen had searched out the very essence of the humanity in both of them, and for no more than a joke, betrayed it.

When Rogan awoke the next morning Rosalie already had breakfast waiting for him. The room had no kitchen, but she used a hot plate to make coffee and had brought some rolls. While they ate she told him that Klaus von Osteen was not sitting in court that day but would be sentencing a convicted prisoner the next morning. They reviewed everything she knew about von Osteen—what she'd told Rogan before he'd gone to Sicily and what she'd learned later. Von Osteen was a powerful political figure in Munich and had the backing of the U.S. State Department for a higher climb to power. As a judge, von Osteen had a twenty-four-hour guard at his home and when he went outside. He was without personal guards only in the Munich Palace of Justice, which swarmed with its own complement of security police. Rosalie also told Rogan about her job as a nurse's aide in the Munich Palace of Justice.

Rogan smiled at her. "Can you get me in there without my being seen?"

Rosalie nodded. "If you must go there," she said.

Rogan didn't answer for a moment. Then he said, "Tomorrow morning."

After she had gone off to work, Rogan went out to do his own errands. He bought the gun-cleaning packet he needed to disassemble and oil the Walther pistol. Then he rented a Mercedes and parked it a block away from the pension. He went back up to the room and wrote some letters, one to his lawyer in the States, another to his business partners. He put the letters in his pocket to post after Rosalie came home from work. Then he took apart the Walther pistol, cleaned it thoroughly, and put it back together again. He put the silencer in a bureau drawer. He wanted to be absolutely accurate this last time, and he was not sure he could get close enough to compensate for the loss of accuracy the silencer caused.

When Rosalie came home he asked, "Is von Osteen sitting tomorrow for sure?"

"Yes." She paused a moment, then asked, "Shall we go out to eat, or do you want me to bring something into the room?"

"Let's go out," Rogan said. He dropped his letters into the first post box they passed.

They had dinner at the famous *Brauhaus*, where the beer steins never held less than a quart and twenty kinds of sausages were served as appetizers. The evening paper, *Tagenblatt*, had a story about the killing of Wenta Pajerski in Budapest. The democratic underground believed responsible for the murder had been smashed by a series of secret police raids, the paper reported. Fortunately, the bomb had injured no one but the intended victim.

"Did you plan it that way?" Rosalie asked.

Rogan shrugged. "I did my best when I booby-trapped the chess piece. But you can never tell. I was worried one of those waitresses might get a stray fragment. A lucky thing Pajerski was a big guy. He soaked it all up."

"And now there is only von Osteen," Rosalie said. "Would it make any difference if I told you that he seems like a good man?"

Rogan laughed harshly. "It wouldn't surprise me," he said. "And it doesn't make any difference."

They didn't speak about it, but they both knew it could well be their last evening together. They didn't want to go back to their room with its green sofa and narrow bed. So they drifted from one great barnlike beer hall to another, drinking schnapps, listening to the happy Germans singing, watching them gulp countless quarts of beer at long wooden tables. The huge Bavarians wolfed links of fat little sausages and washed them down with towering, frothy steins of golden beer. Those who were momentarily sated fought their way through thick, malt-reeking crowds to the marbled bathrooms, to make use of the special vomiting bowls big enough to drown in. They vomited up all they had consumed, then fought their way back to the wooden tables and clamored for more sausages and beer, only to return to the bathrooms and get rid of it once again.

They were disgusting, but they were alive and warm, so warm their heat made the huge beer halls hot as ovens. Rogan kept drinking schnapps while Rosalie switched to beer. Finally, having drunk enough to be sleepy, they started walking to their pension.

When they passed the parked Mercedes, Rogan told Rosalie, "That's the car I rented. We'll take it to the courthouse tomorrow morning and park it near your entrance. If I don't come out you just drive away and leave Munich. Don't come looking for me. OK?"

"OK," she said. Her voice was tremulous, so he held her hand to keep her from crying. She pulled her hand away, but it was only to take the key from her purse.

They entered the pension, and as they mounted the stairs she took his hand again. She released it only to unlock the door to their room. She entered and switched on the lights. Behind her, Rogan heard her gasp of fright. Seated on the green sofa was the Intelligence agent Arthur Bailey; closing the door behind them was Stefan Vrostk. Vrostk held a gun in his right hand. Both men were smiling a little.

"Welcome home," Bailey said to Rogan. "Welcome back to Munich."

CHAPTER 18

Rogan smiled reassuringly at Rosalie. "Go and sit down. Nothing is going to happen. I've been expecting them." He turned to Bailey. "Tell your fink to stash his weapon and you do the same. You're not going to use them. And you're not going to stop me from doing what I have to do."

Bailey put away his gun and motioned to Vrostk. He said to Rogan very slowly, very sincerely, "We came to help you out. I was just worried that maybe you'd gone kill-crazy. I thought you might just start blasting away if you found us here, so I figured I'd get the drop and then explain."

"Explain away," Rogan said.

"Interpol is on to you," Bailey said. "They've hooked you up with all the murders, and they're processing copies of all your passport photos. They traced you to Munich; I got the Teletype in my Munich branch office just an hour ago. They think you're here to kill somebody, and they're trying to find out who. That's the only thing you've got going for you. That nobody knows who you're after."

Rogan sat on the bed opposite the dusty green sofa. "Come off it, Bailey," he said. "You know who I'm after."

Bailey shook his head. His lean, handsome face took on a worried look. "You've become paranoiac," he said. "I've helped you all along. I haven't told them anything."

Rogan leaned back on the pillow. His voice was very calm. "I'll give you this much credit. At the beginning you didn't know who the seven men in the Munich Palace of Justice were. But by the time I came back you had a dossier on every one of them. When I saw you a few months ago, the time you came to tell me to lay off the Freisling brothers, you knew all seven. But you were not going to let me know. After all, an intelligence network operating against the Communists is more important than an atrocity victim getting his revenge. Isn't that how you Intelligence guys figure?"

Bailey didn't answer. He was watching Rogan intently. Rogan went on. "After I killed the Freisling brothers you knew nothing would stop me. And you wanted Genco Bari and Wenta Pajerski knocked off. But I was never supposed to get away from Budapest alive." He turned to Vrostk. "Isn't that right?"

Vrostk flushed. "All arrangements were made for your escape. I cannot help it if you are a headstrong person who insists on going his own way."

Rogan said contemptuously, "You lousy bastard. I went by the consulate just to check you out. There was no car waiting, and the whole neighborhood was crawling with cops. You tipped them off. I was never supposed to get to Munich; I was supposed to die behind the Iron Curtain. And that would have solved all your Intelligence problems."

"You're insulting me," Bailey said. "You're accusing me of having you betrayed to the Communist secret police." His voice held a tone of such sincere outrage that Rosalie glanced doubtfully at Rogan.

"You know, if I were still a kid in the war you would have fooled me just now. But after the time I spent in the Munich Palace of Justice I see through guys like you. I had you all the way, Bailey; you never fooled me for a second. In fact, when I came to Munich I knew you'd be waiting, and I thought of tracking you down and killing you first. Then I figured it wouldn't be necessary. And I didn't want to kill someone just because he got in my way. But you're no better than those seven men. If you'd been there you'd have done what they did. Maybe you have. How about it, Bailey? How many guys have you tortured? How many guys have you murdered?"

Rogan paused to light a cigarette. He looked directly into Bailey's eyes when he started to speak again. "The seventh man, the chief interrogator, the man who tortured my wife and recorded her screams, is Judge Klaus von Osteen. The highest-ranking federal judge in Bavaria. The politician with the brightest future, maybe the next chancellor of West Germany. Backed by our State Department. And in the pocket of the American Intelligence apparatus. So you can't afford to have him killed by me, and you certainly can't have him arrested for war crimes."

Rogan stubbed out his cigarette. "To keep me from killing von Osteen, to keep the story of his being a Gestapo man a secret, I had to be destroyed. You ordered Vrostk to betray me to the Hungarian secret police. Isn't that right, Bailey? Simple, airtight, cleanhanded, just the way you sincere Intelligence types like it."

Vrostk said in his arrogant-sounding voice, "What is to stop us from silencing you now?" Bailey gave his subordinate a weary look of impatience. Rogan laughed.

"Bailey, tell your fink why he can't," Rogan said, amused. When Bailey remained silent Rogan went on, speaking directly to Vrostk. "You're too stupid to figure out what I've done, but your boss knows. I've sent letters to people in the States I can trust. If I die, von Osteen will be exposed, American diplomacy will be discredited. American Intelligence here in Europe will get it in the neck from Washington. So you can't kill me. If I'm captured—same thing. Von Osteen will be exposed, so you can't inform on me. You have to settle for breaking even. You have to hope that I kill von Osteen and nobody ever finds out why. I won't insist on your helping me. That would be asking too much."

Vrostk's mouth hung open in shock. Bailey stood up to go. "You've got it figured out pretty good," he said to Rogan. "Everything you said is true, I won't deny it. Vrostk took his orders from me. But everything I did was part of my job, to get my job done. What the hell do I care about your getting your revenge, getting your justice, when I can help our country control Germany through von Osteen? But you've made all the right moves, so I have to stand aside and let you do what you have to do.

And I have no doubt that you'll get to von Osteen, even though there'll be a thousand cops looking for you tomorrow morning. But you've forgotten one thing, Rogan: You'd better escape after you kill him."

Rogan shrugged. "I don't give a damn about that."

"No, and you don't give much of a damn what happens to your women either." He saw that Rogan had not understood. "First, your pretty little French wife that you let them kill, and now this *fraulein* here." He jerked his head toward Rosalie, who was sitting on the green sofa.

Rogan said quietly, "What the hell are you talking about?"

Bailey smiled for the first time. He said softly, "I mean that if you kill von Osteen and then you get killed, I put your girl through the wringer. She gets accused as an accessory to your murders, or she gets put away in that insane asylum. The same thing happens if von Osteen lives and gets exposed by your letters after you're dead. Now, I'll give you an alternative. Forget about killing von Osteen and I'll get you and the girl immunity for everything you've done. I'll get it fixed so the girl can enter the States with you when you go back. Think it over." He started to leave.

Rogan called after him. His voice was shaky. For the first time that evening he seemed to have lost some of his confidence. "Tell me the truth, Bailey," Rogan said. "If you had been one of the seven men in the Munich Palace of Justice, would you have done the things to me that they did?"

Bailey considered the question seriously for a moment; then he said quietly, "If I really believed it would help my country win the war, yes, I would have." He followed Vrostk out of the door.

Rogan got up and went to the bureau. Rosalie saw him fit the rifled metal of the silencer on the spine of the Walther pistol and said in an anguished voice, "No, please don't. I'm not afraid of what they'll do to me." She moved toward the door, as if to stop him from going out. Then she changed her mind and sat on the green sofa.

Rogan watched her for a moment. "I know what you're thinking," he said, "but didn't I let Vrostk and Bailey get away with trying to kill me in Budapest? Everybody in that profession is some kind of special animal, not a human being. They're all volunteers; nobody forces them into those jobs. They know what their duties will be. To torture, betray, and murder their fellow human beings. I don't feel any pity for them."

She did not answer; she bowed her head into her hands. Rogan said gently, "In Budapest I risked my life to be sure no one else was hurt except Pajerski. I was ready to give up everything, even my chance of punishing von Osteen, so that none of the innocent bystanders would be injured by me. Because those bystanders were innocent. These two men are not. And I won't have you suffer because of me."

Before she could answer, before she could raise her head, he went out of the room. She could hear his footsteps going swiftly down the stairs.

Rogan drove off in the rented Mercedes and turned onto a main avenue, his foot pressed down on the gas. At this hour there was little traffic. He was hoping that Bailey and Vrostk didn't have their own car, that they had come to the pension in a taxi and would now be on foot and trying to catch another taxi.

He had gone no more than one block on the avenue when he saw them walking along together. He drove on one more block, then parked the car and started walking back along the avenue to meet them. They were still a hundred feet away when they turned into the entrance of the Fredericka Beer Hall. Damn, he thought, he'd never be able to get at them in there.

He waited outside for an hour, hoping that they would have a few quick beers and then come out. But they did not reappear and he decided, finally, to go inside.

The beer hall was not full, and he saw Bailey and Vrostk right away. They had a long wooden table to themselves and they sat there gobbling down white sausages. Rogan took a seat near the door, where he would be shielded from them by a full table of beer drinkers who were still going strong.

As he watched Bailey and Vrostk drink, he was surprised at their appearance and behavior, and then amused at his surprise. Till now he had always seen them when they wore their masks of duty, careful not to reveal any weakness. Here he saw them relaxed, their disguises put aside.

The arrogant Vrostk evidently loved fat women. Rogan saw Vrostk pinch all the plump waitresses and let the skinny ones go by untouched. When a really hefty girl passed him, carrying a tray loaded with empty beer steins, Vrostk could not contain himself. He tried to embrace her, and the glasses went flying all over the wooden table; the waitress gave him a good-natured push that sent him staggering into Bailey's lap.

The lean Arthur Bailey was a finicky glutton. He was devouring plate after plate of white sausages, leaving a little stringy tail of casing from each. He washed each mouthful of sausage down with a gulp of beer. He was totally absorbed in what he was doing. Suddenly he lunged toward one of the bathrooms.

Vrostk followed him, weaving drunkenly. Rogan waited a moment; then he, too, followed. He went through the doorway and was in luck; Bailey and Vrostk were the only occupants.

But he could not shoot; he could not take his Walther pistol from his jacket pocket. Bailey was bent helplessly over one of the huge white vomit bowls, puking up everything since breakfast. Vrostk was gently holding Bailey's head so that it would not dip into the bowl's contents.

Caught with their defenses down, they were curiously touching. Rogan backed out before they could see him, and left the beer hall. He drove the Mercedes to the pension, parked it, and went up to the room. The door was not locked. Inside Rosalie was sitting on the green sofa, waiting for him. Rogan took off the silencer and threw it back into the bureau drawer. He went and sat beside Rosalie on the sofa.

"I couldn't do it," he said. "I don't know why, but I couldn't kill them."

CHAPTER 19

Next morning, while he drank his coffee he wrote down the name of his lawyer in the States and gave it to her. "If you do get into any kind of trouble, write to this man," Rogan said. "He'll come to help you out."

That he had not killed Bailey and Vrostk had in some way resigned Rosalie to Rogan's hunting down von Osteen. She did not try to make him change his mind; she accepted what he had to do. But she wanted him to rest for a few days. He looked ill and very tired. Rogan shook his head. He had waited too many years; he did not want to wait another day.

He had a slight headache. He could feel pressure on the part of his skull covered by the silver plate. Rosalie gave him water to wash down the pills he always carried with him. She watched him check the Walther pistol and put it in his jacket pocket. "Aren't you using the silencer?" she asked.

"It makes the gun too inaccurate," he said. "I'd have

to get within fifteen feet to be sure of hitting him. And maybe I won't be able to get that close."

She understood what he really meant: that he had no hope of escaping; that it would be useless to silence the murder weapon. Before they went out the door she made him hold her in his arms, but there was no way he could comfort her.

He had her drive the car, not trusting his uncertain lateral vision at an important time like this. His damaged optical nerve was at its worst in moments of stress, and he wanted to be able partially to shield his face with his hand as he moved through the city. Munich would be full of police looking for him.

They drove past the courthouse steps, through the square Rogan remembered so well, with its florid columned buildings. Rosalie parked the Mercedes a short distance from the side entrance. Rogan got out of the car and entered the majestic archway into the courtyard of the Palace of Justice.

He walked over the cobblestones that had once been stained with his blood and whose crannies had swallowed the tiny blasted fragments of his skull. Stiff with tension, he followed Rosalie into the emergency medical clinic and watched her slip into her white nurse's tunic. She turned to him and said quietly, "Are you ready?"

Rogan nodded. She took him up an interior staircase that led into a dark cool hall floored with marble. Great oak doors studded the sides of the corridor at intervals of fifty feet, the doors to the courtrooms. Deep niches next to each door contained suits of armor. Some of the niches were empty, the armor looted during the war and not yet replaced.

As he passed the courtroom doors Rogan could see the accused—petty thieves, burglars, rapists, pimps, murderers, and innocents—waiting for justice. He walked down the long corridor, his head pounding with the fearful emotion that filled the air like a malevolent electric current. They came to a wooden stand that held a placard: *"Kriminalgericht,"* and underneath: *"Bundesgericht von Osteen, Präsidium."*

Rosalie was pulling at his arm. "In this courtroom," she whispered. "Von Osteen will be the middle one of three judges."

Rogan went in past a bailiff and took a seat in a back row. Rosalie sat beside him.

Slowly Rogan raised his head to look at the three judges on their platform at the lower end of the huge courtroom. A spectator seated in front of him obscured his view, and he tilted his head to get a better look. None of the judges looked familiar. "I don't see him," he whispered to Rosalie.

"The judge in the middle," she whispered.

Rogan stared intently. The judge in the middle bore no resemblance to von Osteen. Von Osteen's features were aristocratic, aquiline; this man's features were lumpy. Even his forehead was narrower. No man could have changed so much. He whispered to Rosalie, "That's not von Osteen; he doesn't look anything like him."

Slowly Rosalie turned to face him. "You mean he's not the seventh man?"

Rogan shook his head. He saw gladness in her eyes

and did not understand. Then she whispered, "But he *is* von Osteen. That's certain. I know that for a fact."

He felt dizzy suddenly. They had tricked him after all. He remembered the Freisling brothers' sly smiles when they had given him the information about von Osteen. He remembered something confident in Bailey's manner when they talked about von Osteen, something that had amused the Intelligence agent. And now he understood the look of gladness in Rosalie's eyes: He would never find the seventh man and so would abandon his search and live out his life. This was what she had hoped for.

The silver plate in his skull began to ache, and the hatred for the whole world that soured his blood drained the strength from his body and he started to slump toward Rosalie. She caught him as he began to black out, and a stout bailiff, seeing what had happened, helped to carry Rogan out of the courtroom and down to the emergency clinic. Rosalie stayed on the side where Rogan had his gun, feeling the shape of it through the cloth of his jacket. In the clinic she made him lie on one of the four beds and put a screen around him. Then she held up his head and pushed the pills down his throat. In a few minutes the color returned to Rogan's cheeks and he opened his eyes.

She spoke to him softly, but he didn't answer, and finally she had to leave him there to attend to someone who had come in for minor medical aid.

Rogan stared at the ceiling. He tried to force his brain to think things out. There was no way the Freisling brothers could have been lying when they put down the same names of their wartime colleagues. And Bailey had admitted that it was von Osteen who was the man Rogan sought. Was it possible, then, that Rosalie had lied to him? No. For Rosalie, it was impossible. There was just one thing to do: Find Bailey and make him tell the truth. But only after he had rested; he felt too weak now. Rogan closed his eyes. He slept for a little while. When he woke up he thought he was in one of his familiar nightmares.

From the other side of the screen came the voice of the chief interrogator who had so long ago tortured him and betrayed his humanity. The voice was powerfully magnetic, ringing with sympathy. It was inquiring after the man who had fainted in the courtroom. Rogan could hear Rosalie, her tone respectful, reassuring the visitor that the man had been overcome by the heat and would shortly be well again. She thanked the Honorable Judge for his kindness in asking after the health of her patient.

When the door closed Rosalie came round the screen and found Rogan sitting up in bed. There was a grim smile on his face. "Who was that?" he asked, wanting to make sure.

"Judge von Osteen," Rosalie said. "He came to ask how you were. I told you what a kind man he was. I always felt he couldn't be the one you were looking for."

Rogan said softly, "That's what the brothers were smiling about, and Bailey too. They knew I would never recognize von Osteen, just as they hadn't recognized me. But his power was all in his voice, and I'd never forget that." He saw her look of dismay. "Is Judge von Osteen sitting this afternoon, after lunch?" he asked.

Rosalie sat down on the bed, with her back to him. "Yes."

Rogan patted her shoulder, his fingers drawing strength from her young body. He could feel the exultant joy running through him. In a few hours it would all be over; he would never dream his terrible dreams again. But he would need all his strength. He told Rosalie what shots to give him from her drug supply in the clinic locker. As she prepared the needle he thought about the change in von Osteen's appearance.

Remembering von Osteen's proud features, Rogan knew the man would not have had voluntary facial surgery merely to escape danger. In the years since they had last seen each other von Osteen had gone through his own hell of suffering. But it didn't matter; nothing mattered anymore, Rogan thought. Before the day was over both their worlds would end.

CHAPTER 20

S uperior Federal Judge Klaus von Osteen sat on the high bench, two fellow judges flanking him. He saw the mouth of the prosecuting attorney move, but he could not make any sense out of the words. Haunted by his own guilt, his own fear of punishment, he could not concentrate on the case before him. He would have to agree with the verdict of his two fellow judges.

A flash of movement in the rear of the courtroom caught his eye, and his heart contracted painfully. But it was just a couple taking their seats. He tried to see the man's face, but the head was bent down and away. Now the defense attorney was listing excuses for his client. Von Osteen tried to focus his attention on what the man was saying. He concentrated. Suddenly there was a commotion in the rear of the courtroom. By a great effort of will von Osteen kept himself from standing up. He saw a woman in white and one of the bailiffs half carry a slumping man out through the doorway. It was not an uncommon occurrence in these courtrooms where people were subjected to such cruel stress.

The incident disturbed him. With a crook of his finger he summoned one of the clerks to the bench and whispered instructions. When the clerk returned and told him that a friend of the nurse employed by the court had fainted and had been taken to the emergency room, von Osteen sighed with released tension. And yet there was something strange about such a thing happening at just this time.

When the court recessed for lunch, von Osteen decided to go down to the emergency room and inquire after the man's condition. He could have sent a clerk, but he wanted to see for himself.

The nurse was a very pretty girl and fine-mannered. He noted with approval that she was far superior to the usual type employed in such government positions. She motioned to a screen around one of the hospital beds and told him that the man was recovering; it had been a mild fainting spell, nothing serious. Von Osteen stared at the screen. He was almost overcome by the urge to walk behind that screen and look into the man's face, to resolve all his fears. But such an act would be extraordinary, and besides, the nurse was in his way. She would have to move aside. He said a few words to her with mechanical politeness and left the room. For the first time since he had become a judge in the Munich Palace of Justice he walked through the courtyard, turning his head so that he would not see the interior wall against which the bodies had been stacked on that terrible day long ago. Leaving the courtyard, he walked down the main avenue where his chauffeured limousine waited to take him to his home for lunch.

The detective guard sat in the front with the chauffeur, and von Osteen smiled with amusement. The guard would be almost no protection against a determined assassin, merely another victim. When the car rolled into the driveway of his home he noticed that his house guard had been increased. They would help. It would force the assassin to make his attempt somewhere else, and Marcia would be safe.

His wife was waiting for him in the dining room. The table was set with white napery that had a faint tinge of blue in the curtained light. The silver sparkled, and the bowls of bright flowers were arranged with the skill of an artist. He said jokingly to his wife, "Marcia, I wish the food were as good as the setting." She made a face of mock displeasure. "Always the judge," she said.

Looking at his wife, von Osteen thought, *Would she believe in my guilt if it all came out?* And he knew that if he denied everything she would believe him. She was twenty years his junior, but she truly loved him. Of that he had no doubts. Von Osteen ran his hand over his face. The surgery had been excellent, the best available in Germany, but close up the many scars and seams in his flesh were clearly visible. He wondered if that was why she kept the rooms curtained against too bright a light and the lamps dim.

After lunch she made him lie down on the sitting room sofa for an hour's rest. She took a seat opposite him, a book in her lap.

Klaus von Osteen closed his eyes. He could never

confess to his wife; she believed in him. And after all, he had received his punishment. A few weeks after *Rosenmontag*, 1945, a shell had fragmented his face. He had always accepted his terrible wound without bitterness, for in his mind it atoned for the crime he had committed against the young American agent in the Munich Palace of Justice.

How could he explain to anyone that as a staff officer, a nobleman, a German, he had come to recognize the degradation of his country, its dishonor. And like a man who is married to a drunkard and who decides to become a drunkard himself to show his love for her, so he, too, had become a torturer and a murderer to remain a German. But had it really been that simple?

In those years since the war he had lived a truly good life, and it had been natural to him. As a judge he had been humane, never cruel. He had left his past behind him. The records of the Munich Palace of Justice had been carefully destroyed; and up until a few weeks ago he had felt little remorse for his wartime cruelties.

Then he had learned of Pfann and Moltke being killed, and the Freisling brothers too. A week ago the American Intelligence officer Arthur Bailey had come to his home and told him about Michael Rogan. Rogan had murdered the men who had been von Osteen's underlings in the Munich Palace of Justice when he had been a judge without the sanction of law. Von Osteen remembered Michael Rogan. They had not killed him after all.

Arthur Bailey had reassured him. Rogan would never accomplish his final murder, American Intelligence would see to that. They would also keep von Osteen's war atrocities a secret. Von Osteen knew what this meant. If he ever came to political power in West Germany he would be subject to blackmail by American Intelligence.

Lying on the sofa he reached out to touch his wife, not opening his eyes. It was only when he learned that Rogan was alive that Von Osteen began to dream about him. He had nightmares of Rogan leaning over him, the back of his skull bleeding, the blood dripping onto von Osteen's face. He had nightmares of a phonograph record blaring out the screams of Rogan's young wife.

What was the truth? Why had he tortured Rogan and then killed him? Why had he recorded the screams of that pretty girl dying in childbirth? And why had he finally betrayed Rogan, led him on to hope for life, led him on to believe his wife was still alive?

He remembered the first day of the interrogation, the look on Rogan's face. It was an innocent, good face, and it had irritated him. It was also the face of a young man to whom nothing terrible had yet happened.

On the same day von Osteen had gone to visit the prisoner's wife and found that she had been taken to the medical room, in childbirth. Walking toward the room, he had heard the young girl's screams of pain, and when the doctor had told him the girl was dying von Osteen had decided to have the screams recorded to frighten Rogan into talking.

What a clever man he had been, von Osteen thought. He was clever in everything. Clever in evilness; and after the war, living with his ruined face, clever in goodness. And being clever, he now knew why he had destroyed Rogan so completely.

He had done so, von Osteen realized, because evil and good must always try to destroy each other; and it must follow that in the world of war and murder, evil must triumph over good. And so he had destroyed Rogan, slyly led him on to trust and hope. And at that final moment when Rogan had begged for mercy with his eyes von Osteen had laughed, his laughter drowned by the roar of the bullet exploding into Rogan's skull. He had laughed at that moment because the sight of Rogan, with his hat tilted forward over his brow, had been genuinely comical; and death itself, in those terrible days of 1945, was merely a burlesque.

"It's time." His wife was touching his closed eyes. Von Osteen rose from the sofa and his wife helped him into his jacket. Then she walked with him to the limousine. "Be merciful," she said.

It caught him unawares. He looked at her, his eyes dazed with incomprehension. She saw this and said, "On that poor wretch you will have to sentence this afternoon."

Suddenly von Osteen had the overwhelming urge to confess his crimes to his wife. But the car was wheeling slowly away from the house on its way back to the Munich Palace of Justice. Already under sentence of death, but hoping for a reprieve, von Osteen could not bring himself to confess.

CHAPTER 21

A rthur Bailey paced the office of the CIA communications center in the U.S. Army headquarters outside Munich. Early that morning he had sent a coded
radiogram to the Pentagon explaining the entire situation
regarding von Osteen and Rogan. He had recommended
that no action be taken by his organization. Now he was
waiting impatiently for the answer.

It was nearly midday before a reply was received.
The clerk took it into the top secret decoding room, and
half an hour later the message was placed in Bailey's
hands. It stunned him. It instructed him to have von Osteen guarded and to inform the German police of Rogan's
intentions. This course of action would be so disastrous,
Bailey thought, that he decided to use the radiophone to
the Pentagon. The code signature on the reply was that of
a former German teammate of Bailey's, Fred Nelson.
They couldn't speak too freely over the radiophone, but
maybe Bailey could get his message across to Nelson.

And he sure as hell had to hurry. Rogan might be right behind Judge von Osteen this minute.

It took him ten minutes to get a connection. After identifying himself he said cautiously, "Do you people know what the hell you're doing with those instructions you sent me? You could blow the whole political setup sky-high."

Nelson's voice was cool and noncommittal. "That decision came from the top in Intelligence. It's been cleared by the State people. So just go ahead and follow orders."

Bailey said disgustedly, "They're all crazy." His voice sounded so worried that Nelson took pity on him.

"That one aspect you're worried about," Nelson said guardedly, "that's being taken care of."

Nelson was referring to the letters Rogan had sent to his friends in the States. "Yes, I understand," Bailey said. "What was done about that?"

"We've kept a file on him since your first report. We know everybody he might correspond with, and we've placed a postal intercept on the post of every person he knows."

Bailey was genuinely surprised. "Can you get away with that in the States? I didn't think of that at all."

"National security. We can do anything." Nelson sounded sardonic. "Will this guy let himself be taken alive?"

"No."

"He'd better not be," Nelson said, and broke the connection.

Bailey cursed himself for having called instead of just following instructions. He knew what Nelson's last remark meant. He had to make sure that Rogan was not captured alive, or not allowed to remain alive after he was captured. They didn't want him talking about von Osteen.

Bailey got into the waiting staff car and told the driver to take him to the Palace of Justice in Munich. He didn't think Rogan had had enough time to make his move, but he wanted to make sure. Then he would pick up Vrostk, and they would both go to the pension and finish Rogan off.

CHAPTER 22

In the emergency clinic of the Munich Palace of Justice, Rogan prepared for his final meeting with Klaus von Osteen. He combed his hair and straightened his clothing; he wanted to look as presentable as possible so as not to stand out in the crowd. He patted his jacket pocket on the right side to make sure the Walther pistol was still there, though he could feel its weight.

Rosalie took a bottle of colorless liquid from her mobile tray and poured some on a thick square of gauze. She put the gauze in Rogan's left-hand pocket. "If you start to feel faint, hold it to your mouth and breathe in," she said.

He bent down to kiss her, and she said, "Wait until he finishes with his court; wait till the end of the day."

"I'll have a better chance if I catch him coming back from lunch. Be in the car." He touched her cheek lightly. "There's a good chance I'll get away."

Sad-eyed, they smiled at each other with pretended

confidence; then Rosalie took off her white tunic and tossed it on a chair. "I'll go now," she said, and without another word, without a backward look, she left the clinic and walked through the courtyard to the street beyond. Rogan watched her before he, too, left the clinic and climbed the interior stairs to the main-floor corridor of the Munich Palace of Justice.

The corridor was filled with convicted people waiting to learn their punishments, and with them were families and friends, as well as the defenders and dispensers of justice. They gradually began disappearing into the individual courtrooms, until the cool dark hall was empty. There was no sign of von Osteen.

Rogan walked down the hall to the courtroom where von Osteen had sat that morning; he was late. The court was already in session, and had been for some minutes. It was ready to sentence the criminal before it. Von Osteen, as president of the court, sat between his two fellow judges. They all wore black robes, but only von Osteen wore the high conical hat of ermine and mink that designated the chief judicial officer, and his figure seemed to exert a dread fascination on everyone in the courtroom.

He was about to sentence the convicted criminal before him. The decision was announced in that magnificent persuasive voice that Rogan remembered so well. It was a life sentence for the poor wretch before him.

Rogan felt an enormous relief that his search was ended. He walked a hundred feet past the doors of the courtroom and stepped into one of the empty niches in the wall of the corridor, a niche that for a thousand years had held the armor of a German warrior. He stood there for nearly an hour before the people in the courtroom came out of the oaken doors into the corridor.

He saw a black-robed figure exit from the courtroom through a small side door. Von Osteen was coming toward him through the shadowy corridor. He looked like an ancient priest prepared for sacrifice, black robes flapping, the conical hat of ermine and mink like a bishop's mitre, holy and untouchable. Rogan waited, blocking the corridor. He drew the Walther pistol and held it before him.

They were face-to-face now. Von Osteen peered through the shadowy light and whispered, "Rogan?"

And Rogan felt an overwhelming joy that this last time he was recognized, that his victim knew the crime for which he must die. He said, "You condemned me to death once."

He heard the hypnotic voice say, "Rogan, Michael Rogan?" And von Osteen was smiling at him and saying, "I'm glad you've finally come." He reached up and touched his furred hat. "You are far more terrible in my dreams," he said. Rogan fired.

The pistol shot clanged through the marble corridors like some great bell. Von Osteen staggered back. He held up both hands as if to bless Rogan. Rogan fired again. The black-robed figure began to sag, the conical hat making the fall majestic, sacrilegious. People ran into the corridor from the adjoining courtrooms, and Rogan fired one last bullet into the body lying on the marbled floor. Then, with the pistol in his hand, he ran out of the side exit into the sunlit square. He was free.

He saw the waiting Mercedes just a hundred paces

away and started for it. Rosalie was standing beside the car, looking tiny, as if she were at the end of a long tunnel. Rogan started running. He was really going to make it, he thought; it was all over, and he was going to make it. But a middle-aged, mustached policeman, directing traffic, had seen the gun in Rogan's hand and rushed from his post to intercept him. The policeman was unarmed. He stood in Rogan's path and said, "You are under arrest; you cannot brandish a weapon in public."

Rogan brushed him aside and walked toward the Mercedes. Rosalie had disappeared now; she must be inside the car starting the motor. Rogan desperately wanted to reach her. The policeman followed him, grasping his arm, saying, "Come now, be sensible. I am a German police officer, and I place you under arrest." He had a thick Bavarian accent that made his voice sound friendly. Rogan hit him in the face. The policeman staggered back, then ran after him clumsily, trying to herd Rogan into the Palace of Justice with his heavy body, yet afraid to use physical force because of the pistol in Rogan's hand. "I am a police officer," he said again, astonished, unable to believe that anyone would refuse to obey his lawful commands. Rogan turned and shot him through the chest.

The policeman fell against him, looked up into his eyes, and said, with surprise, with innocent horror, "O wie gemein Sie sind." The words rang in Rogan's mind. "Oh, how wicked you are." He stood there, paralyzed, as the policeman fell dying at his feet.

Frozen in the sunlit square, Rogan's own body seemed to disintegrate, the strength running out of it. But then Rosalie was beside him, taking his hand and making him run. She pushed him into the Mercedes and then roared out of the square. She drove wildly through the streets of Munich to reach the safety of their room. Rogan's head had tilted to the right, away from her, and she saw with horror a trickle of blood seeping out of his left ear, the blood running against gravity, propelled by an inner pump gone awry.

They were at the pension. Rosalie stopped the car and helped Rogan get out. He could barely stand. She took the soaked gauze out of his left jacket pocket and held it to his mouth. His head jerked up and she could see the scarlet snake of blood trickling from his left ear. He was still clutching the Walther pistol in his right hand, and people in the street were staring at them. Rosalie led him into the building and helped him up the stairs. The spectators would surely call the police. But for some reason, Rosalie wanted him behind closed doors, shielded from everybody's eyes. And when they were alone and safe she led Rogan to the green sofa and made him lie down and put his head in her lap.

And Rogan, feeling the ache of the silver plate in his skull, knowing he would never dream his terrible dreams again, said, "Let me rest. Let me sleep before they come." Rosalie stroked his brow, and he could smell the fragrance of roses on her hand. "Yes," she said. "Sleep a little."

A short time later the Munich police entered the room and found them so. But the seven men in the high-domed room of the Munich Palace of Justice had finally killed Rogan after all. Now, ten years later, his damaged brain had exploded in a massive hemorrhage. Blood had poured from every aperture of his head—from his mouth, his nose, his ears, his eyes. Rosalie sat quietly, her lap a basin filled with Rogan's blood. As the police came forward she started to weep. Then slowly she bowed her head to bless Rogan's cold lips with a final kiss.

ABOUT THE AUTHOR

The son of Italian immigrants who moved to the Hell's Kitchen area of New York City, **Mario Puzo** was born on October 15, 1920. After World War II, during which he served as a U.S. Army corporal, he attended City College of New York on the G.I. Bill and worked as a freelance writer. During this period he wrote his first two novels, *The Dark Arena* (1955) and *The Fortunate Pilgrim* (1965). When his books made little money despite being critically acclaimed, he vowed to write a bestseller. *The Godfather* (1969) was an enormous success. He collaborated with director Francis Ford Coppola on the screenplays for all three *Godfather* movies and won Academy Awards for both *The Godfather* (1972) and *The Godfather, Part II* (1974). He also collaborated on the scripts for such films as *Superman* (1978), *Superman II* (1981), and *The Cotton Club* (1984).

He continued to write phenomenally successful novels, including *Fools Die* (1978), *The Sicilian* (1984), *The Fourth K* (1991), and *The Last Don* (1996).

Mario Puzo died on July 2, 1999. His final novel, *Omerta*, was published in 2000.